THE DOPEMAN'S *fine ass son*

NASTEE

Published by Author Nastee

contents

disclaimer

If you're new here… then you don't know about my disclaimers. If you've been here, you already know how I'm coming. When reading my disclaimers, please understand MY PERSONALITY DEMANDS that I just… keep it a band and be myself lol.

This read is predictable than a muhfucka. I DID NOT WRITE THIS FOR SHOCK VALUE, LOL. This book was written from my heart and my brain, to entertain, not to make you be like… "oh shit, I CAN'T BELIEVE THIS." My books are full of things that might trigger you, and I don't know what that means because what triggers you might not trigger me and vice versa, however, if you're adverse to identity issues, domestic violence, loss, drugs, guns, violence, suicide attempts, starting over, lies, betrayal, etc… then just know, this book got all that!

Furthermore, THIS BOOK DO HAVE A CLIFFHANGER. Not it DOES have a cliffhanger. IT DO have one, lol. THIS BOOK IS A 3-PART SERIES WITH A DEVELOPING SPIN OFF SERIES! But, if you like this book, I promise I'll release book 2 soon BECAUSE IT'S ALREADY DONE!

Also, this is a re-release from my former catalog. If you've read this before, just smile and share it, lol.

Stormeisha (Black Girl Tired BookTok)
Jazzy (The BookTok Rookie)
Shaunee (AudreyShanice)
Bewticious (B. Bewtie)
Shanny (BIH_IREADBOOKS)
Dosey-Dose (DoseofQ)
Lil' Baby AKA Jack- Jack (Resourcefulbooks)
Tash AKA Twinny (Tashtheauthor)
Arie My Personal Thelma

The ENTIRE Boozy Book Baddies Community
BookTok
My Facebook Group: The Reading Chamber
Bookstagrammers

If I've forgotten anybody, please charge it to my head, and not my heart. There are many names playing through my head right now, lol.

CHAPTER 1

Cocaine laid on the bed at the dusty Motel 8. He couldn't afford to be seen by anyone who may know him, or worse, want him dead.

"Yeah baby, suck that shit up," he said to his thick thighed and almost overdosed lover. She was gone off that coke and Cocaine.

Trisha pushed her hair out of her face as Cocaine poured another line across the crease of his pelvic area and sprinkled some of that white girl on the tip of his dick. Trisha giggled and took herself to ecstasy as she moved from left to right, snorting it up, and then stuck her tongue out and licked what was on his dick. By this time, Cocaine was already in his dream world, reliving the same memory he did every day; the day his father was murdered...

"What I tell you, boy? Keep ya' head up and walk with confidence. You a muthafuckin' king, but ain't nobody gon' just treat you like one. How do you reign?"

"Strong, long, and hard. Prosperously, abundantly, adamantly. Break bread with those who can't break bread for themselves, but never break my back to serve the loaf to the one who's back was never broken."

"Exactly, that's my boy. Come on, Coco."

"Where are we going, Dad?" ten-year-old Cocaine asked his father as they stepped out of an all-white Bentley with the taupe leather seats and white interface.

"To show you your destiny. You need to see this."

Though his father had always affectionately called him Coco, he was named Cocaine after the drug because other than money; it was the only other thing his father loved in this world. His mother died in childbirth with him, and all he had was his father. Cocaine was the prince of the streets of Houston. His family handled the drug game, money laundering, and their murder game was on lock. Many feared Juaqeen, Cocaine's father, but many adored him. He was a sight to behold. His rich, dark chocolate overflowed like a fondue fountain. His white teeth shone brighter than the sun even on its hottest day. His body was tight, and he was lean, even to be in his forties. Cocaine took after his father in every aspect. He loved his pops, and he would do anything for him, and vice versa.

Cocaine stepped into the warehouse with his father. It was a large, abandoned building on the outskirts of town that held a secret his father hadn't shown anyone, but he knew he could trust Cocaine. His son was not only his heir but his best friend oftentimes. Cocaine looked around, and though the building was empty, he knew something amazing was hidden behind the large gated double doors he saw up ahead of him. He ran to them, excited to see what was behind them. His father laughed and ran up behind him, jingling the keys to the lock on the gate and then to the door behind them.

"You ready, Coco?"

"Hell yeah, dad. I mean, yeah, dad."

"Watch ya' mouth boy," he said as he gave him a menacing look. Coco began to shrink down into his clothes afraid of how his father's temper may react that day because he could go a little crazy

sometimes. But instead, Juaqeen gave him a sweet smile and rubbed his hand across Coco's wavy head.

When Juaqeen opened the door, the sound of a gun popping alerted Juaqeen. He instinctively stood in front of Coco, protecting his son from the present danger. He then drew his gun as he stood in front of his son, waiting for someone to pop out, but Coco remembered what his father had taught him...Hiding in plain sight is easier than hiding, so Coco snuck off to the right side where there were boxes that would shield his person while allowing his father to scope the spot out. Coco looked at his dad, feeling the finality of the situation, something inside of him just knew this was going to go sideways. He mouthed the words, "I LOVE YOU," to Juaqeen, and Juaqeen was almost able to say it back, but not before gunshots rang out.

Pop! Pop! Pop!

The gunshots were loud, and Coco hated to admit it, but he was afraid. His father fell to the ground near him. Coco wanted to run out, to help his father, but Juaqeen turned his head in his direction, and his eyes said NO! Coco kept trying to move toward him, but every step he took, his father's eyes became more intense. Even though Juaqeen was hurt, Coco had never been more afraid of his father at that moment. It could have been the reverence he felt for him or the fact that he felt his father was invincible, but he would find out this day, that his father was not. Suddenly, Coco heard footsteps approaching him. The shoes tapped loudly against the floor, almost rhythmically.

"Mmm...Juaqeen, I finally caught you slippin', and here I thought you were immortal."

"I am! I'll forever live on, bitch boy," Juaqeen laughed as he spit blood from his mouth. He'd been shot three times. Once in the chest, once in the leg, and another in the arm.

"Unless you got nine lives, nigga, yo' ass is dead!"

Juaqeen smiled to himself before he met his fate. In his eyes, he would live forever through Coco. He was an immortal in the way of leaving behind a legacy, and not even the man who stood atop of Juaqeen could take that away from him. Cocaine sat there on the ground, crying hoping the man did not find him. He could see the man, but the man could not see him. His gun went off one last time, sending Juaqeen to where all ghetto king's go, Thugs Mansion, leaving Cocaine to be raised by servants and the streets.

The last thing Cocaine saw every time he closed his eyes was the man who killed his father...He was large, at least 6'5, all gold teeth, and he had a gorilla tattooed on his face, which meant he was part of the gorilla gang, one of the main territories his father ran.

He knew one day...he would get his revenge, and it was that exact reason he was in Nashville, Tennessee. Trisha's giggling brought Cocaine out of his thoughts.

"What you laughin' at?" Trisha turned around and stuck her fingernail in her mouth seductively.

"I'm laughin' at you."

"Why?" Cocaine asked as he rose from the bed.

"Because you been zonin' out this whole time we been here, you must be high."

What Trisha didn't know was Cocaine wasn't just fucking her because she was fine. He had a plan to his madness. Cocaine didn't even get high, at least not off coke. He was high on revenge, and the lust of that was more than enough.

Trisha giggled again, and Cocaine rose from the bed.

"I'ma give you somethin' to laugh about, girl," he growled as he grabbed her by the hips and pulled her down on the bed closer to him. He whipped his glorious, rock hard dick out that glistened from Trisha's saliva, and she shimmied her ass into his pelvis, hoping he was going to fuck the shit out of her. Quickly, he rammed his wet dick into her tight, gushy pussy, grabbing her hair.

"Yeah, you want this dick, don't you?"

"Yes, Cocaine! Fuck!" she yelled. In her mind, she thought about how she'd met him earlier that night and how they couldn't keep their eyes off one another. She had to have him, and now that she was, she wasn't sure if she could handle it.

"Tell me you want this dick, Trisha," Cocaine roared as he threw his dick into her.

"I want your dick, Cocaine! Oh my God!"

"Mhmm….you want somethin' from me, and I want somethin' from you…"

"What do you want from me, daddy?" Trisha asked as he kept pushing his big dick inside her guts.

"I need info," he groaned as he kept fucking her.

Trisha looked over her shoulder and slid up from his dick a little.

"What kind of info?"

"I thought you wanted this dick!"

"I do!"

"Then get yo' ass back here!" Cocaine pulled Trisha back on his shiny dick and fucked her harder than he'd ever fucked anyone.

"Aghh! Cocaine! Yes, fuck this little pussy. Blow my back out!"

"Yeah, you like that, then tell me where yo' boss at!"

Trisha turned around to look at him, and he turned

her head back around and choked her from behind. Trisha exclaimed with pleasure.

"COCAINE!" He kept beating her and asking her the same question with each stroke.

"Where's. Your. Boss?"

"Shit! Shit, I'm 'bout to cum! He's…he's…at his restaurant in Green Hills at Johnathan's Grill!"

Cocaine couldn't help himself anymore. Hearing the location of the man who killed his father made his balls tingle, and his kids spilled inside of her effortlessly. Cocaine had specifically chosen her for the night so he could get information from her. After getting a tip in Texas that the man who had killed his father was in Nashville, he didn't give it a second thought. He came straight away. He was hoping to stop at a bar, get a drink, and lounge for the night, and then tomorrow he could do some reconnaissance, but when he saw the gorilla tattooed just behind her ear, the same exact design as the man from sixteen years ago, he knew it was fate. He was destined to run up on that nigga.

As he came, and it was a long one, he reached into his pocket and pulled out a wad of money and threw it up in the air. When it came down, it landed right on her back, which made her leak more of her love juices onto his fat manhood. Cocaine smacked her on the ass and pulled out of her and went into the bathroom to clean up. When he came back, Trisha was gone, but his phone was unlocked and lit up. He picked up his phone and read the message she'd texted inside.

"I didn't need hush money, the dick was just fine. Text me sometime." She closed the message with a winky face. Cocaine knew she was the cool type of chick, and maybe, just maybe if he needed her again, she would come through and help him out. He couldn't lie, her pussy was lowkey good, but you know what Tupac said, 'Revenge is like the sweetest joy next to getting pussy,' but it was so much sweeter and so much better. Cocaine's dick got hard again, it always did whenever he thought about what he would do when he got his hands on that gorilla nigga. The gang had changed so much, the gang that his father singlehandedly started had turned its back on the royal family, and if it was the last thing Cocaine did, he would avenge his father, take back over the streets, and make his father's dream of immortality come true.

"Dear Lexxy, I laid your dress across the bed. Meet me at the restaurant at 7. I love you, baby. Tonight is going to be special."

Lexxy put the note against her chest and moved from side to side in excitement. She knew she was supposed to be having dinner tonight with Lucky, but now that he was saying it was going to be something special, she was extra hype. She looked at the dress on the bed, and it was perfect for her, and definitely poppin' for a special occasion. It was a liquid silver, with the droopy back and it tied around the neck. She had the perfect shoes to go with it, and it was going to set off her cascading chocolate skin. Lexxy slid out of her pajamas that she'd been wearing for most of the day after she took a shower. She put the dress on and ran her stiletto nails against the fabric, letting it melt against her skin.

Her hair was in a messy bun, and she figured she'd keep it like that for her date tonight with her man. She and Lucky had been together for five years, and if it was as special as she thought it was, she was going to be getting engaged tonight, so she made sure to go light on the jewelry as to not overdo it when she got her ring. Lexxy wasn't a big makeup wearer, so she put on her foundation and made her highlight glisten like her pussy would.

After she was dressed, she looked at herself one last time in the mirror in the hallway. Her long, thick legs and wide hips had her feeling herself a little too much, but she deserved it. Lexxy was a medical student, and graduation was close. So every time she looked at herself, she always pictured herself in a white lab coat, about to doctor some shit up. She didn't see a beautiful twenty-six-year-old. She saw hard work and accomplishments. Lexxy grabbed her keys and headed for the door, but as she opened it, there was a man standing in front of her door.

"Hello ma'am, my name is Tony, I'll be your driver for this evening," Tony said as he tipped his hat and held out his hand for Lexxy to take it. She smiled as she walked down the stairs of her house.

Yeah, I'm gettin' that ring tonight, she thought as she slid into the all black Escalade with tinted windows.

When Lexxy got to the restaurant, Tony came around and opened her door. She'd never been here before, but she couldn't wait to eat. The sign at the top of the building said Puckett's, and it was downtown, so she knew the inside would be fancy.

Tony ran up to the door and pulled the door open so she could walk in. The inside was decorated with bright, white lights, and the staff was smiling at her and whispering, only confirming her suspicions of a proposal tonight.

Lucky was her world, and she couldn't wait for them to be together forever. This had been coming for a long time. She was patient and stayed down, even against her mother's advice, so this had to work out. She couldn't be looking stupid in front of her family.

Lexxy announced her name to the hostess, and she led her to the very back into a secluded room with the chef. This was something Lexxy had always dreamed of because she'd seen it on so many movies. She couldn't believe Lucky remembered.

"Hello, beautiful," Lucky said as he ran his fingers up the spine of her back, admiring the dress he got for her. He kissed her on the cheek as she climbed onto the barstool.

"Hello, handsome. This is amazing!"

"I know," Lucky admitted, knowing he was showing off.

"So, what's the special occasion?" Lexxy asked as she looked around the room. The chef was setting up to cook in front of them, and he was pouring their wine into two flute glasses. This had to be it.

"You'll see, be patient beautiful."

Lucky licked his pink lips, and Lexxy took a second to admire his handsome physique. He was 6'2 with light-brown eyes, his skin was smooth, gold like honey dreads that he kept in braids, a tailored black suit with the Gators to match. .e was looking so good.

As the evening continued, they talked, laughed, ate, and drank almost two bottles of wine. Lucky realized

Lexxy was getting lit, and he didn't want the surprise to be ruined. He gave the chef a look that signaled for their plan to commence. The chef nodded, and three men with violins came out. Lexxy spun around in her seat as the men approached her, and she smiled. This was going perfectly. The men were playing her favorite song, 'A Thousand Years,' by Christina Perry. She remembered once telling Lucky that she wanted to walk down the aisle to this song, and she couldn't believe he remembered since men often forgot important things.

"Baby, you remembered!" Lexxy squealed as she threw her arms around Lucky's neck, and he kissed her softly on the cheek. In his mind, this was a night he hoped she would never forget.

"Of course I did, beautiful. You're my queen."

Lexxy smiled as she continued listening to the beautiful song playing before her. Lucky came around the side, sneaking up on her, and he dropped to the floor on one knee with a box in his hand. Lexxy's hands flew to her mouth as tears began to well up in her eyes.

"Baby, you know I love you," Lucky started as the music faded into the background.

"I would do anything for you, and tonight, I wanna do something for you. You stayed down and by my side when I didn't have shit. You helped me pay for school, and I love you for that. I can never repay you for everything you've done for me, so tonight, I wanna ask you if you'll..."

"Yes! Yes, baby! Yes, of course!" Lexxy jumped out of her seat. She couldn't hold it in anymore. She was busting with happiness.

Lucky smiled and opened the box, and Lexxy's happiness quickly ended when she saw what was inside. Instead of the four -carat diamond ring, she'd showed him several times at Tiffany's...it was a key, a rusty, old, brown key.

"Are you fucking kidding me, Lucky? A house key?"

"Yeah, I'm asking you to move in, I thought that was what you wanted."

The violinists had completely disappeared, and the chef was wrapping up in embarrassment. He felt bad for the beautiful woman who was expecting a ring.

"'I thought this was what you wanted, baby?"

Lexxy took a few steps back; she was about to let it rip on his ass.

"Lucky, you fucking idiot! Five long years I've waited for you to get serious, five long fucking years, and a key is all I'm worth? How could you do this to me? What is your problem?" Lexxy asked with anger rumbling in her belly. She was now feeling like an idiot. The night she thought was special for her ring finger, and her life was nothing more than a dull expression of 'love' from Lucky.....

After the dinner turned into an epic fail, Lexxy just wanted to go home. Unfortunately, it was Lucky's weekend to stay with her, and she knew no matter what, he wouldn't deviate from that, no matter how mad she was at him. When they got in the car to leave the restaurant, Tony wasn't the driver, Lucky was, and she hated having to sit right next to him. Every few minutes, she found herself looking over at him, mugging the shit out of him and rolling her eyes. She felt hate in her heart in this moment, and the love she had grown for Lucky over the years flew out the window, literally. She rolled down the window in an angry stupor and threw the house key she'd taken out of the box out the window. She even heard the 'tink' sound it made when it hit the ground as they drove down the interstate.

"Lexxy, come on, baby. It's not that big of a deal, why you trippin'?"

"I guess I'm just being 'crazy' right? Fuck you, Lucky! Picture this, me at home getting ready for this special evening, thinking you're finally ready for us to be together and be happy, and then boom, you pull out a fucking house key. Are you slow, or am I retarded?"

Lucky pulled the car over right on the interstate and looked right at Lexxy. He couldn't for the life of him understand why she thought it was a big deal. For him, this was a major deal. It had been five years since he and Lexxy had been dating, but he'd been peeping her since before he ever approached her. Lucky knew if he was going to pull Lexxy, he was going to have to have something going for himself, and the only thing he had at the time was a job, where he was working as a telemarketer for a phone company, and he had his own place.

Lucky grew up in a single parent home, with his father. He was raised that women were the root of all evil, but if you called all the shots, you not only made the rules, but set the tone for the entire relationship, so that was what he had been doing with Lexxy. He'd been with women on and off, but Lexxy, she was something special.

Lucky approached her one day at her car. His work building was on the same parking lot that most of the college students parked their cars at. They allowed the students to park there given they advertised the telephone company's logo on their car. Lucky would watch her every day get in and out of her car, as one of her classes was at the same time he had to be at work. She just looked like she was about something. Lexxy didn't carry herself like most of the other women he knew. She looked smart, was conservative, and she wasn't glued to her phone like most of the women he saw, but she was also beautiful. Not that Instagram fine, but truly gorgeous. Unfortunately, as time passed, he hoped Lexxy didn't want to get serious, but she did, so to him, getting serious meant calling her his girlfriend, letting her have a drawer or two at his house, and now, giving her his house key. He wasn't ready for marriage, nor did he ever know if he would be.

"Lexxy, tell me what you want me to say, and I'll say it. I love you, and I don't want our special night to be ruined."

Lexxy exhaled a deep breath, exasperated with the conversation and the fact that he still didn't understand what the problem was. She shook her head and threw her hands up. She didn't want to talk about it anymore, and she damn sure didn't have any more energy to give to the situation.

Realizing he had been defeated, Lucky got back on

the road and continued to drive to Lexxy's house. When they pulled up, Lexxy all but ran in the house. She wanted to make sure she slammed the door in his face, so he knew she wasn't playing. She was sick of playing his games, and he needed to realize that.

The door almost shattered she closed it so hard. Lexxy began replaying the events of their relationship in her mind. She'd paid for him to go to school for Christ's sake. He still wasn't using the bachelor's degree he earned in English. She felt like she had completely wasted her time.

When she got in her room, she began undressing and preparing for bed. She ripped her dress off, almost tearing the fabric through her dress in her closet. She'd slipped out of her shoes at the door, leaving them in front hoping Lucky would trip over them in anger, but when she heard the door close, and him walk up the stairs immediately after, her plan had failed. She grabbed a t-shirt and a pair of Lucky's boxers and slipped them on. She climbed into the bed, throwing the covers over her head. Doing her best not to break down into tears.

Lucky came into the room, the tension in the air was so thick not even a knife could cut it.

She breathed deeply, hoping he'd believe she was on her way to sleep, even though she wasn't. She was honestly too pissed off to sleep, there was no fucking way she'd be able to drift off, not now, and Lucky knew that. But Lucky was an idiot, he wasn't done with the conversation.

"Lexxy, I'm not lettin' you go to bed—"

"Shut up, Lucky! You know the last five years ain't

been all cake and fucking ice cream, but I keep holding out and holding out waiting for you to fucking step up. I've always let you take the lead in this relationship. I've always gone at your pace and tried not to force myself on you, and even when my mother told me to leave your stupid ass alone, I didn't because I love you! So here's how this shit is gonna go, you're going to marry me, or at least put a ring on my finger, if not, we're done!" Lexxy said as she flipped the covers over her head, giving Lucky a death stare.

Lucky ran his fingers across his head, letting down his dreads from the beautiful braids they were in, and he took a deep breath. He was starting to feel like Lexxy was getting out of control, the main thing his father always said not to do, so he had to put her back in check before things went farther than they had already gone.

"Look, you ain't gon' force me into no marriage, Lexxy. So you do whatever it is you feel like you need to do. Stay with me or don't, that's a choice you gotta make."

Lexxy's eyes bulged out of her head; she couldn't believe what she was hearing. After five years, he still hadn't figured it out, and even in the midst of them probably breaking up, he was holding true to his own. Lexxy huffed and disappeared back under the covers. Her heart was breaking for the love she felt for Lucky and the stupidity that she had dealt with all of this time with him.

CHAPTER 3

A few hours later, Lexxy's phone began ringing, and as bad as she didn't want to answer it, she felt like she didn't have much of a choice. It was her best friend Denny G. It was two o'clock in the morning, and she figured if she was calling this early, something must be wrong.

"Hello?" Lexxy answered, frustrated that she hadn't gotten any sleep.

"Girl, I got a mad hangover. I'm supposed to be at work in an hour, but I don't think I'm gon' make it in, bitch. You got me?"

Lexxy looked over at Lucky who was peacefully sleeping, but she didn't give a damn. Normally, she would wake him up and ask if he was cool with her taking a shift, but she didn't care what he thought or how he felt, so she made the decision herself. Though Lexxy didn't need a job because her family was rich, she enjoyed working for the things she had. When she graduated high school, she got a job at a diner downtown, called the Sunshine Diner, and she loved her job. Serving people wasn't fun, but she loved the people she met, it was always something interesting going on there, and as she went to school, she took less and less shifts. Besides, it wasn't like she needed the money, she just enjoyed the social activity.

"Yeah, that's fine. I'll get up now and head that way. Bitch, quit drinkin' so much," Lexxy laughed before she hit the end button. Lexxy wondered what Denny had been up to. She hadn't heard from her all day, and she couldn't wait to tell her bestie about the ring she thought Lucky was giving her, but since it went sour, she was glad she didn't even have the chance to tell her about the date in the first place. She hated the way people talked about Lucky. She knew for herself what was going on in her relationship, and she didn't want to hear about it every time she talked to Denny. So she had stopped telling her their business, and even though she loved Denny, she didn't take advice from her. If it was up to her, Lexxy would have had three jump offs by now, and she wasn't that type of person. Lexxy's parents had been together since she was born, always married, and always happy, and that was what she wanted. She wanted a happy, committed relationship. Not this bullshit that the 21st century put together as a façade of happiness.

Lexxy gently pulled the covers off of her and slid out of bed and went to her closet to get out her work uniform, a yellow dress with a white collar and white shoes. The diner was very old school, a Nashville treasure, something else that Lexxy loved about her job, it was historic.

Lucky had left the light on in the bathroom before he got in the bed, something Lexxy normally complained about, but right now, she was thankful because she wouldn't have been able to see otherwise in her room.

She stepped into the bathroom and reached for her toothbrush to brush her teeth. As she powered on the mechanical device, she looked at herself in the mirror and realized she wasn't ugly, nor was she stupid. So she couldn't figure out why for the life of her she kept waiting for Lucky to get it right. He wasn't her only choice, well at this point he was just because she wasn't the cheating type, but she could have any man she wanted, so why was she so stuck over Lucky? He wasn't the first man she'd ever been with, nor was he her first real relationship, but it was something about him. Maybe it was the normalcy she experienced with him. Her parents always tried to introduce her to rich, obnoxious men, and that wasn't what she wanted. She just wanted to be with someone who was grounded and down to earth because even though she'd been raised in a lifestyle where your pockets determined your wealth, she wasn't like that at all. It somehow skipped her in the gene pool.

After Lexxy brushed her teeth, she rinsed her face off with water and went back into her room to get dressed. Lucky still hadn't moved from his spot, he was sleeping effortlessly. Meanwhile, Lexxy was feeling like shit on the inside. She was experiencing a spiritual warfare inside of her, and Lucky looked like a brand new shiny penny. She hated how handsome he was; it made it that much harder to hate him.

Lexxy took her hair down and put it back up into a high ponytail. The messy bun was cute to go out in, but it often was unmanageable at work, so she tried to clean it up a bit. She took one last look at a sleeping Lucky, and then she headed downstairs to grab her keys and get out the door. Then she remembered she was about to graduate if she was able to pass her exams, so she needed to study a little more. She grabbed her textbook that sat on the mantle over the fireplace and headed out the door to clock into work. Lexxy figured it wouldn't be that busy at work, at least not this early. Many people slept on the small diner because it was tucked away behind several buildings, so it presented the perfect chance for her to study.

Cocaine going to Johnathan's Grill was a complete bust. He didn't find the man he was looking for, and he refused to spend his money in his establishment, so after scoping the place out and even going into the hidden spots, he left. On his way back to the hotel, his stomach rumbled, making him realize he forgot to eat, so he wanted to stop and get something real quick. Unlike Houston, everything in Nashville closed fairly early, so if he wanted a meal that would fill him up, he'd have to go somewhere and sit down.

As he got close to the Motel 8, he saw the bright lights of the Sunshine Diner, and he could smell the crisp bacon in the air. His stomach had been talking to him for a full thirty minutes now, and he couldn't wait any longer. He pulled his car over and parked it on the street, putting some change in the meter, and then going inside the building.

When he opened the door, he noticed the woman at

the counter with her nose deep in a book. He figured she'd be with him in a minute, so he went ahead and sat down and took a look at the menu. He felt like he'd walked into the 50's, but it was nice, and it was low-key. That was the most important thing to him. It was hard to survive in the jungle if everyone noticed you or saw who you were.

He looked over the two-sided menu, realizing that all of his options came with eggs and bacon, so he could order just about anything. He was finally ready to place his order, so he held up his hand and called out to the woman across the counter, who in ten minutes, still hadn't noticed him. He then wondered if she was deaf, which wouldn't be unheard of, or even more so, it wouldn't be that surprising, he wasn't discriminative. He loved all kinds of people, and he appreciated a hard worker.

A few more minutes passed by, and he still wasn't waited on, so he went up to the counter and stood in front of the girl, trying to read the words upside down of what she was reading. Cocaine reached his chocolate hand across the counter and stuck his hand in the middle of her book. She looked up and smiled.

"I'm sorry, can I help you?"

Until then, he hadn't noticed how beautiful she was. He was surprised to see such a pretty woman working in a place like this. He leaned a little closer so he could read her name tag, and he smirked.

"Yes, Ms. Lexxy, I've been trying to get your attention for some time now. How are you?"

"Oh, I'm alright. I'm sorry, I was studying. Can I get you something to drink?"

"I'm ready to order if that's ok with you."

Cocaine licked his bottom lip revealing his simple but very shiny grill on the bottom row of his teeth.

"Oh, of course. I'm sorry, what can I get you?"

"You can start by killing the apologies. I'm sorry for coming in and disturbing your studying process, beautiful. Let me get an Arnold Palmer, this bacon, egg, and waffle slider with my eggs scrambled with cheese, and that'll be a—"

Cocaine's sentence was interrupted by Lexxy's glasses falling from her face. She often wore them to work and school, or if she was going to be reading or in front of a computer, which was pretty much all the time, except for at night when she was at home.

Cocaine stuck his hand out and grabbed the glasses quickly, not wanting them to bounce off the counter and hit the floor, and when he saw her deep, brown eyes, his insides started melting. He felt like he could get lost inside of her eyes. The windows to her soul were speaking loudly to him, and he wanted to answer, but he was trying to be respectful and not like every other nigga in the world who had probably tried their hand with her.

"Oh, God, I'm sorry."

"What I tell you about bein' sorry, baby? You ain't got nothin' to apologize for," he said as he handed her back her glasses. Lexxy's beautiful dark skin began blushing as Cocaine's hand brushed across hers when he handed her the glasses back. She slid them back onto her face and turned around to put the order in.

Cocaine didn't want to do too much, but he couldn't help himself. When Lexxy walked away, he found his eyes wandering down the back side of her body, looking straight at her legs, and it wasn't her ass that fucked his mind up. It was something around her, glowing. Cocaine didn't believe in the stars and shit, and an aura that burned bright, but Lexxy was making him question that.

Lexxy leaned over the bar that connected to the kitchen and gave the cook the order. Since the night didn't seem like it would be too busy, Lexxy and the cook were the only two employees there, and they were the only ones that needed to be.

"Ok, I just put your order in, so it should be out soon. Can I get you anything else while you wait?"

Cocaine turned over her textbook that had a picture of a skeleton on the front of it, and he grinned.

"Yeah, you can give me some conversation since you didn't pay me any attention when I walked in. What's your major?"

Lexxy's cheeks blushed a cherry red as she answered him.

"I'm in medical school."

Cocaine had never met anyone in medical school, let alone anyone who truly made it past their freshman year in college, so he was amazed.

"I don't mean no disrespect, but….why would you be working in here and you're in medical school?"

Lexxy loved being able to give an answer to something like this. She knew what people who knew her thought about her, and the people who didn't seem to get what she had to say.

"The entire time I spent in my parent' 'house was a very guarded and sheltered life. My parents have a pretty good amount of money, so I always went to the best schools, had the best clothes, and was around what others would assume were 'the best' people. It's because of that lifestyle that I've been able to see the truth about how people can be. I've been able to see what people look like and what they do, and I always wanted to give back. I didn't want to be one of those trust fund kids that I grew up with, and I knew a lot of them. I wanted to stand on my own two feet, and I wanted to blend in with society. I'd always stuck out, and I was tired of that. I wanted to live a normal life, so right after high school, I got a job here, and I've never left. Weird, right?"

"Nah, it's anything but that. It's kind of sexy, Ms. Lexxy."

Cocaine liked what he was hearing from this young woman. It had been a long time since he met someone who was academically smart. He was used to hoodrat, dirty hoes, but this was surprising. This diner, that seemed so simple and like a hole in the wall was now a special treasure that he stumbled upon.

CHAPTER 4

Cocaine's food came out ten minutes later, and Lexxy brought it over to him along with a glass of water.

"If that'll be all for you, for now, I'm gonna go back to the counter and hit the books some more. I've got an exam, and this is the most studying I've done in a few weeks."

Cocaine understood, and he didn't want to interrupt Lexxy. Besides, he was hungry, so he would wait until he was done eating to interrupt her again, and he fully planned to.

While Lexxy studied, Cocaine's eyes were drawn to her essence, to her being, to everything about her. He had never met anyone as chocolate as he was unless they were family, and he'd never been with a chocolate woman before, but he would break all the rules for Lexxy. Each bite he put in his mouth was bittersweet as he watched Lexxy. He knew when his food was gone he'd have no reason to still be in the diner, except for HER. He wanted to talk to her, to get to know more about her. Lexxy was surprisingly the most interesting person he'd ever met in his life, and he could say that with full confidence.

Once he finished eating, he grabbed his plate and dirty napkins he used and placed his glass on his plate and carried it over to the counter where Lexxy was.

"I could've gotten that for you. It's really no problem."

"It may not be, but we can't let the future of medicine fall behind, now can we?" Cocaine said as he reached across the counter and grabbed Lexxy's hand. Instantly, it was like electricity went through her hands and up her spine, making her tingle all over. For a second, she forgot about Lucky and what he wasn't doing. She forgot that she had a whole man at home that in a few hours, would be getting up and going to work and probably calling her to apologize.

"I don't know about the future in medicine, but yeah, I guess so."

"Good. If you're not sure about what you're studying about, I'd be happy to quiz you, you know, to see what you do know and what you need to study harder on."

Then it hit her. She remembered Lucky's face after realizing she was being flirted with. It had been so long, the concept almost seemed foreign to her. In the first year of Lexxy and Lucky's relationship, men flirted with her left and right, but it was always embarrassing and unwarranted, but after she put it out there for the world to know, and everyone knew, that they were together, men suddenly stopped paying her attention. She often heard that she had the 'taken' look, which never bothered her, but now that Cocaine was flirting with her, ooh wee, she had to step back and cut this off before it went too far. She didn't want to hurt his feelings, but even more so, she didn't want to pretend like she was about to do something like this. Like she was really about to give this guy some play.

"Well, while I appreciate that, I'm gonna have to decline. I don't think my boyfriend would like another man helping me in that way, but thank you."

"Boyfriend? I don't care about ya' nigga, baby. If he cared that much about ya' schoolin', he would be here right now while you're at work. I would be here with you until you got off making sure you got all your studying done and that you were taken care of. Hell, I'd get back there and run them orders for you if I had to, but I'm just a different type of nigga, what do I know?"

Lexxy wondered where this handsome stranger came from. She'd met plenty of men in her life, but none were quite as straightforward as this man was. What was this man's name? She realized he hadn't even introduced himself. She also noticed the way his grill gleamed in the light and his muscular body and chocolate skin looked like butter had melted all over it. He was truly a sight to behold. Lucky was handsome, but Cocaine was too damn fine. He had Lexxy's heart doing summersaults, something Lucky hadn't made her do in years. Lucky was familiar, what she was used to, but she also loved him with every fiber in her body, and after that stunt he pulled, seeing another handsome man who was clearly interested in her and awoke such feelings inside of her, she should be ready to run into his arms, but she wasn't.

"Well, I care about my boyfriend, Mr...."

"Cocaine," he said quickly. Her reaction to it was fast as she doubled over in laughter.

"No, really, what's your name?" she asked, holding her side as she tried to contain the laughter that was spilling from her mouth.

"That's really my name. My father named me Cocaine. See, other than money, Cocaine was his favorite thing, so he named me after the thing that helped turn him into the king he was. I ain't used to nobody raggin' on me about my name, Ms. Lexxy."

She instantly stopped laughing after hearing the word was. She figured something must have happened to him, but she didn't want to ask. She wouldn't reach out like that, not to a complete stranger. Instead, she offered him her condolences.

"I'm sorry about your father—"

"Don't sweat it. It's all good. My father is a legend, and I'll honor him in every way I can. Most people would change their name, but not me. I'm proud that he named me after something that he loved. Most parents name they kids stupid shit, or worse, give their kids their father's last name. A father who will never recognize them, and that ain't me, so I'm not ashamed, baby, and you ain't got nothin' to be sorry about. He died a real nigga."

Lexxy had never been talked to like that before. She realized he probably wasn't the most legit guy just by the way he looked. She hated to stereotype, but it was true, and now, after hearing his name, she realized that couldn't have been more true. She didn't want to ask about what he did for a living because it was honestly none of her business, no matter how badly she wanted to know. She was interested in Cocaine, which was the exact reason she had to get away from him, so she didn't fuck up whatever it was she had going on with Lucky because she knew how he could be. Lucky was a crybaby when it came to other men, and she didn't even want to hear his mouth because she didn't like secrets, and she told him everything, even the things she probably shouldn't or that most women wouldn't tell their man.

"And you ain't gotta try to put me off by telling me you got a man, baby. I don't give a damn about ya' man because you lookin' at the future whether you realize it or not."

Lexxy grabbed his plate and glass and turned around to take them back to the kitchen. While she was putting everything in the sink, she tried to gather herself. She didn't want to keep this man on her brain, but she couldn't help it. He seemed genuinely interested in her, and he hadn't been disrespectful by watching her strangely or looking at her for long periods of time. Or even worse, ogling her breasts. He was being polite, gentleman like, well as much as she had seen in another man in a while, but he was pushing it, and she didn't really want him to stop.

"Listen, Cocaine, you're sweet, but I can't even entertain you in that way. I have a man, and he don't play them type of games."

Cocaine felt laughter rumble in his belly and eventually erupted through his mouth.

"I'm sorry, baby, I ain't tryna laugh at you, but the simple fact that he don't play them type of games ain't got nothin' to do with me and got everything to do with you. He knows what he got, and he ain't tryna lose it. I feel that baby because I'm tryna see what that's like, and I ain't even talkin' about what's inside your panties. I wanna fuck your brain," Cocaine said as he stood up from the counter and grabbed Lexxy's hand. He placed a small kiss on it, letting his lips linger a few minutes too long before Lexxy finally snatched her hand away.

She longingly watched him walk out the door, and something about him made her think if staying with Lucky was the right thing. Not because he was a terrible boyfriend, or because Cocaine was so amazing, but simply because she was confused and conflicted on what she was supposed to be doing with Lucky. What if she really had wasted the last five years of her life on a nigga who didn't really deserve her in the first place?

Cocaine didn't want to leave, but the truth was he had moves to make, and even though he found himself temporarily distracted, he wouldn't allow that to happen again unless Lexxy was going to become his woman. He was so intrigued by her that the entire time they spoke, he could see little fantasies of them in his mind. Cocaine always got what he wanted, no matter what it was. If it was a car, he got it, a woman, he got it, a house, he fucking got it.

The sun was finally coming up over the Nashville skyline, the Batman building was highlighted in its wake, and Cocaine had someone to meet. He had planned to meet the realtor later on in the afternoon, but while he was in the diner, he received a text from her that stated she could meet him to show him a few of the houses early, around six a.m. He appreciated her discretion and privacy, he was paying her enough, so after or before hours care could be and should be expected.

Cocaine couldn't keep on staying in that damn hotel. He was used to having a house, and he missed his home in Texas, but now, he had to settle a score. He needed to make Nashville his home as well if he planned on taking the streets back from the gorilla gang. Those niggas were runnin' around actin' like monkeys, totally embarrassing his father's name. He couldn't wait to get his hands around the man who ruined his life or tried to anyway, and rip the streets away from him.

That was fifteen years ago when his father passed away, and the streets that were his birthright were usurped from him, but it was cool. He had fifteen years to get over it and come up with a plan that would make his father proud, and keep him in business.

Cocaine drove back toward the Green Hills area. Trisha had tipped him off to the neighborhood that her boss lived in, and his realtor, Suzanne. He also called her Dirty Susie because of the glasses she wore in her profile picture on her website, and she had found a few listings in the area.

Dirty Susie texted him the address of the house that was in the same exact neighborhood as the man he was looking for. Of course, Dirty Susie didn't know that, but it was all the same to Cocaine.

As he pulled into the neighborhood, he began looking for the description of the house Trisha had given him. She told him the iron gates encased the entire house, and that would be a big sign that he was looking at the right house. There was nothing special about the gorilla man's house, just that it was way, way in the country, and no one could see the house because it was covered by trees. It was the trees that had the excitement, considering they had apples coming out of the leaves.

The further Cocaine drove, he started to give up on finding the house. Even though he had given Trisha the best dick, she would ever have in her life, that didn't mean she had to be loyal to Cocaine. She could have been trying to set him up for all he knew. He hoped it wasn't so because he always kept a choppa and his sexy Beretta tucked away for just in case. He didn't believe in harming women unless it was killin' the pussy, but he would do more to her than kill that pussy if she betrayed him.

Cocaine drove as far as he could through the neighborhood, and when he was about to give up, he finally saw the red apples hanging from the tree as he was coming over the hill of the street. He slowed down the car, making sure not to stop completely, but going slow enough so he could get a good look, and it was true; he couldn't see the house, only the gates, the trees, and the very top of what seemed like it could be a house.

Cocaine looked at it and committed it to memory. If the house in the neighborhood worked out, he was going to buy it and start stalking his prey immediately. As he looked at the address Dirty Susie had texted him; he realized the house was just a few houses up from the apple tree house. This couldn't have gotten any better. His revenge was just a few houses away, and he hoped like hell he could stick to his plan and make some shit happen. After all he had been through and all he had done, he deserved this. He needed this.

"Ok, Armond. I'm out of here. You good?"

"Yeah, Sam and Lucy just clocked in, you're good to go."

Lexxy said goodbye to Armond and took off the apron she'd had to wear the last hour of work. It was starting to get busy, and she hated for her uniform to get too messy from all the food she'd deliver, or spill in her case.

As Lexxy walked out the door, she felt good. A calming feeling came over her as she walked to her car. Before she left the house, she was still somewhat mad at Lucky and heartbroken. But now, after being flirted with and having a good conversation, she was feeling herself. The weight of her relationship wasn't as heavy as it had been. She felt pretty good and was excited to go home. Cocaine flirting with her only made her miss Lucky more, but she wished that Lucky still took an interest in her school work the way Cocaine did. Lucky didn't ask her how school was anymore, and she didn't think he didn't care, she just figured it was routine, and he was with her every day anyway, so he probably knew how her day went without her even saying anything.

Lexxy's drive home was smooth and easy; she beat

the early morning traffic by taking the back roads so that she wouldn't be stuck in the terrible Nashville traffic. When she pulled up to the house, Lucky's car was gone. He must have left for work already, even though he usually would text her and say he was leaving, but he didn't. She thought that was because of the strange fight they had the night before. She tried her best not to read too much into it because she could get a little crazy when she did. She didn't want to overreact, something Lucky accused her of often, and she didn't want to embarrass herself. So she went into the house with a clear head and hoped for the best.

She set her keys down on the mantle along with her textbook and headed upstairs. Her door was closed, which was strange, but again, she didn't want to think anything about it. She wanted to just try to keep it cool as always.

When she opened her door, she realized her drawers were open, Lucky's drawers, and they were empty. Her head immediately started swimming with thoughts that could only mean the worst was happening. She went over to her dresser and noticed a white piece of paper that came from the notebook she kept on her nightstand. She picked the note up and began reading it. It was in Lucky's handwriting, so she knew it wasn't some ransom note, something she had seen before, but that's another story.

"Lexxy,

I love you, and you know I do, but I can't and won't be forced into something. We've been together for five years, and we've been happy, but I don't want to get married. You should be with someone who will eventually marry you, someone who will give you what you feel it is you need, and right now I don't think that's me. I think a little time, and separation will do us some good. I'm sorry it has to be like this, but you can't force someone into something. I didn't want to ruin your night at work. I noticed your uniform was gone, so I assumed that's where you went, so that's why I didn't want to send this to you in a text or call you and make you rush home. I love you, forever…and I'm sorry."

The note in Lexxy's hand was now crumbled up in-between her fingers. She held the balled up sheet of paper so tightly she felt like she could've incinerated it with her anger. She was so mad and so hurt. How could he do this to her? He was acting like she'd done something wrong like she was the one who didn't want to commit to him. Was her forcing him to make a decision that bad? She thought for sure that he would make the right choice…her. She knew Lucky loved her, she never questioned that, but what the fuck was holding him back? Five years of her life were now wasted. She'd given him her all, her everything! She didn't even have it inside of her to cry she was so angry. The only thing she could think about was letting it 'Burn,' like Usher, and that was what she was going to do.

Letting the paper crumple up wasn't enough, she never wanted to see the paper or any of the other belongings he'd left ever again. Though he'd taken most of his things, he'd still left several pairs of underwear, a few watches, some of his clothes, and several of his other personal belongings. She never wanted to see them ever again. As Lexxy's mind continued to turn, she thought about Waiting to Exhale and how Bernadette seemed to have been set free by burning her husband's shit, and she wanted to do the same. If Lucky didn't want to be with her, and if he wanted time, she would give them the necessary separation he so desired, and she did so by starting a fire in her gas stove. She was going to stick everything inside, and just burn it the fuck up. She didn't think about the consequences that would have on her. She didn't care.

Through her rage, she couldn't see anything except the fiery blaze. She gathered all of his things and put them in the oven after it was heated, she could see the flames in the bottom of the stove it was so hot. She threw everything in and closed the door, and cut the light on inside so she could see it burning, becoming nothing, just ash.

After a while, she couldn't take watching it anymore. It hurt her heart, and she was dying on the inside. Now she was starting to wish she listened to her mother and even Denny. They'd both told her several times she was too good for Lucky, and he didn't deserve a queen like her. Lexxy never saw it that way. How could she? She loved him blindly and acceptingly. She loved him unconditionally, and she didn't care if others didn't. Whatever he did was her cross to bear, and she had been carrying it every day, no matter how heavy it got, but now, that it was over, she didn't feel any relief. She thought she would, but she didn't.

An hour or so passed by, and she found herself on the couch crying herself to sleep. Why wouldn't she? She'd worked the morning shift, had an emotional evening with her man, and now, Lucky was gone, and that was tiring enough.

She lie on the couch, missing Lucky, seeing him in her mind, wishing she had the power to will him to come back home, but she didn't. The only way she figured she could see him was in her dreams, so she drifted off, hoping Lucky would appear to her…in the form of a loving man. The man she thought he would eventually become.

Lexxy was sleeping so peacefully, or at least she thought she was, she didn't realize she was actually unconscious. She'd forgotten to turn the stove off, and the house was burning into a crisp around her. Luckily, the neighbors saw the flames and called 911 in case someone was inside. Her neighbors knew her car was outside, so they figured she was home. She was so young, they didn't want to see anything happen to the young girl.

Lexxy had often helped the people in the neighborhood as they were elderly. She went grocery shopping for them, checked on them when they weren't well, and she was acquainted with their families as they were hers. To them, they wouldn't just be losing another person in their neighborhood, but a family friend as well.

The ambulance arrived along with the Nashville Fire Department and the Metro Police. They needed all the help they could get to control the fire.

"NFD, is there anyone in here?" one of the firefighters asked after they kicked the door in and began scanning the house to find the place where the fire started.

"Over here, boss!" one of the firefighters called out to the chief. They'd found Lexxy passed out on the couch, her heart rate was slow, almost to the point of death. One of the men picked her up and carried her outside as the other firefighters began putting the fire out. They got her onto a gurney, and the EMT's tried to get her to wake up, but nothing worked. Fluids, chest pumps, nothing. Was Lexxy a goner?

They got her into the ambulance and pulled off as soon as everyone was secure inside. The EMT's continued to monitor her vital signs as they drove. There was a woman in the back with beautiful blonde hair, and she began looking at the ID the firefighters were able to find in the house.

"Lexxy? Lexxy, can you hear me?" She flashed the light in her eyes, and she was still nonresponsive. The blonde woman couldn't help but see how beautiful Lexxy was, and young. She was just a bit older than her, but she realized that that could be her, and she desperately wanted to save Lexxy's life.

"Go faster! We might lose her!" she yelled out to the driver, and he stepped on it, bobbing and weaving through traffic. Carefully, the driver sped through the city streets, and secretly, he was hoping the same, that they could save the beautiful young woman in the back of their ambulance.

Several hours passed by, and Lexxy was finally awake. She'd suffered severe smoke inhalation, and her lungs were ready to shut down. If they hadn't got her to the hospital when they did, she might not have made it. In normal hospital fashion, they contacted her next of kin and emergency contact. Luckily, she was in the same hospital she was born in, so they had all of her records. She was studying to be a doctor, so they knew her well, and they knew just who to call.

Unfortunately, Lucky was the first to show up, and when he did, he was irate. Instead of feeling sorry for her or even worried, he immediately started going in on her. When she could have visitors, he busted in the room asking a million questions.

"What the hell, Lexx? What were you thinking? You burned my shit up in the stove? The house is mad damaged. You could've been killed!"

"It's nice to see you too, ex-boyfriend," Lexxy said through coughs and in a low voice.

"Don't do that shit right now. Here I am worried about your stupid ass, and you want to joke."

"Stupid? I'm stupid? No, you're stupid! What a fucking punk you are. You left me a fucking note, Lucky, a breakup note! I guess you're not at fault though. Of course not, you never do anything wrong!"

Lexxy's blood pressure machine started beeping, indicating that Lexxy was stressing and running up her blood pressure.

"Just go! Get the fuck out of here. You're stressing me the fuck out, and I don't need that right now, so get out!"

Lexxy used all of the strength she had in here to yell at him. She was the one in pain, the one who was going through something, and of course, Lucky acted like he was the one that this happened to. As Lucky left, Lexxy rolled over on her side and closed her eyes. She just wanted to forget about the day and about everything that Lucky had done.

Two days had gone by, and Lexxy was still bedridden. She had no idea what she was going to do about housing. She refused to go back to her parents' house. They'd try to keep her captive or they'd try to make a case about how this was what happens when you step out of the safety of family, and she didn't want to hear that.

Lexxy lie in bed thinking about how just three days before, she was so happy and in love. She thought she was on her way to a proposal, but she wasn't, and now she had no man, no house, and several burns from where the smoke ate away at her skin. It didn't matter to her though; every time she looked at the marks they just reminded her why Lucky wasn't the one.

Denny G had come to visit her while she was in the hospital, and she finally had to break down and tell her best friend the truth, even though she didn't want to. She didn't want to have to tell her friend anything as ammunition for her to hurl it back at her, but what else did she expect? She knew how Denny was, and she wasn't the type to hold her frustration in nor her annoyances with other people. Though Denny didn't always say it with love, that's where it was coming from… her heart.

Denny and Lexxy had been best friends for the last ten years. They met in high school when the then Denise came to her school on a scholarship and Lexxy was on the welcoming committee. Lexxy loved Denise from the moment she met her. She was loud, rude, tactless, and she didn't care about money, that only attracted Lexxy to her more.

Instead of going to prom with boyfriends, they went with one another. They'd always been close, almost like sisters, so whenever Denny said something to Lexxy about her personal life, she took it to heart. Because who knows you, and what you deserve better than your best friend? Nobody!

Though Lexxy was tired of lying in bed, she was hardly well enough to move around, and her doctor encouraged her to rest as much as she felt she should before she was discharged, which would be in the next day or so. She tried to ease her mind and think of something that made her happy, something that made her feel good inside, so she closed her eyes and thought back to the last time she was with Denny, and they were out at a club. She remembered the way it felt to dance and cut loose. She'd taken a hard test that day, and Denise wanted to take her out to celebrate. Lexxy found herself caught up in her thoughts, but her door swung wide open, and a man walked in.

"Alexxis! Tell me exactly what happened, right now!" Her father walked in the room, yelling, as always.

"I'm ok. See?" she said as she sat up in bed showing

her father that despite the hospital gown and several bandages, she was ok.

"No, you're not ok! Where's that nappy headed nigga Lucky? Why isn't he here with you? You can't be out here exposed like this, baby," her father said as he neared her bedside.

Lexxy's parents had never met Lucky; they'd only seen him in pictures or heard him through the phone. Lucky was too afraid to meet her parents because he felt that would be just another thing in the serious department he wasn't prepared to handle.

Lexxy's father already didn't take her seriously, so she didn't want to tell him the truth, but she was a grown woman and could make her own decisions. Hell, she had her own damn insurance, so she could do whatever the fuck she wanted and handle business the way she saw fit.

"He's not here, Daddy. We broke up."

"So you burnt the house down? Damn, Lexxy. You can get in your feelings can't you?"

"I wasn't 'in my feelings' Daddy! I was pissed off because of something he did. He left me after I gave him an ultimatum. I wasn't trying to burn the whole house down, just his stuff. I fell asleep on the couch, and the fumes from the gas knocked me out. It's as simple as that."

Lexxy's father looked at her with intense eyes, thinking of what he should say. On one hand, he was mad at her because if she wanted something done to Lucky, he could've had that taken care of, fuck burning up his shit, he would've had him burned up. Money and respect could make anyone do anything, especially for

Lexxy's father, Dutch. On the other hand, he just wanted to hold his baby girl and tell her that Lucky was never the one, and he wasn't right for her and how he was missing out on a good thing, but no matter what he said, it wouldn't heal his baby's heart, and it wouldn't make her feel any better about what she was going through.

"You have every right to be pissed! But don't be fucking up your shit over a man. Now listen, I came to check on you and make sure you were ok. I love you, and just want what's best for you, always remember that. Wild Bill is going to be standing guard. I've already spoken with the police; it's been ruled as an accident. You know you can go to jail for arson, but it's fine. When are they releasing you? I suspect you'll be coming home. I'll have Rena get your room ready."

"Daddy, relax. I'm not coming home. I've made other arrangements," she lied.

"Tell Rena not to worry. I'm fine, and I don't need my room made up. Where's mommy?"

"Your mother is still out of the country waiting to hear back from me. Are you sure you don't want to come home?" her father asked as sympathy and worry spread across his face.

"I'm an adult, and I have my exams in a week. I need to be somewhere I can focus and get comfortable. Thanks anyway, Daddy."

Dutch gave her a small smile and leaned down to kiss her on the cheek, and then he left without saying another word. As the door was just about closing, Wild Bill walked in the room with his hands behind his back.

"How's uncle's baby? You feelin' ok?" Wild Bill asked

as he entered the room. Wild Bill was Dutch's best friend, and he had always been in Lexxy's life, so much so, she always called him her uncle, and she was truly spoiled by him.

Lexxy immediately perked up when she heard her uncle's voice. He always knew how to make her feel better.

"Wild Bill! Daddy said you were here, but I didn't think you'd be coming in here to check on me," she lied. She always liked to make herself seem modest around her uncle. He still viewed her as a little kid and pretty innocent. What people didn't know about Wild Bill was he had that name for a reason. He was crazy, certifiable. That man was out of his fucking mind, and he had put in major work for Lexxy's family. Saying he was a murderer didn't even explain half of how crazy he was. He was the type to chop your body up and mail each part back to the family one by one, year after year. Just when you thought you were over the loss of a loved one, he came back full throttle and ruined some shit. Lexxy had seen him do it. She wasn't blind to the fact that he wasn't all the way right in the head, but she loved him just the same. He was always compassionate and loving towards her, so she had no reason to ever feel threatened by him.

"Now you know I had to come in here and check on my baby girl. Next time you wanna get rid of a nigga, call me, don't try that shit yourself," Wild Bill laughed as he put his hand on Lexxy's. Wild Bill looked crazy. He had that deranged look in his eyes all the time like he was always ready for some shit to pop off. Even with that strange look, he was still very handsome. He was a big man, not fat, just big. He had hazel eyes that reminded most people of cats, he was tatted all over his body, and he had permanent gold teeth. He kept his hair in a short, curly fro, and it just meshed in with his honey-colored skin. He was very handsome, just off the chain.

"Well thank you for coming to check on me. I appreciate it."

"No problem, anything for you, baby girl. Now, I'ma be outside standing guard of your door. I ain't lettin' nobody else in here unless you ok it. Cool?"

"Of course. The only other person I can think of who would come is Denise. Speaking of which, I need to call her and let her know when I'm getting discharged and let them know I may not be coming in for a few days," Lexxy said more to herself than anyone else.

"Fuck that job, baby girl. You don't even need it for real, but I know why you work it. You've always been a good little helper, and I can't knock you for that. If anything, it makes me love you more. Now get you some rest, and I'll be right outside if you need anything."

Lexxy smiled at her uncle as he exited the room. Since she had been up for a few hours, she was feeling tired, but she needed to make sure she called Denise and then her job before she passed back out. Since her father's visit, she realized she needed to stay with Denise. Staying at home would've only made her miserable, and she didn't want that. She was already starting to feel lonely, and staying with Denise would also allow her the same level of freedom she was used to. She wouldn't have to tiptoe around the house whenever she wanted to leave, and her uncle wouldn't be following her around acting as security for her.

She couldn't get out of bed, so thank God her phone was right on the table beside her. She reached over and grabbed her phone and told Siri to call Denise.

"Calling Denise," Siri said. Lexxy loved her iPhone. The shit came in handy when she needed it.

"What up, babes? You ready to come home?"

"Not yet, but tomorrow or the day after, the doctor said. Have you talked to Sam about me not being able to make it in for a few shifts?"

"Yeah, he said it was cool and that he understood. Your dad called me too and said it was my fault that you still hadn't broken up with Lucky before this shit even popped off."

"Oh my God, are you serious? That man has to be stopped. I don't know why he's always in my business. I love him, but damn, sometimes he crosses the boundaries. When is he going to realize I didn't try to do this to Lucky, I was tryna let his ass go," Lexxy said, exasperated by the entire situation. Her father would often call Denise. She was like family after all, but damn, this was a bit much at this point.

"Don't be mad at him. You know how much he cares about you. Be glad your daddy gives a damn. You already know how mine is, I'm not about to get into that with you today. On another note, a much happier note, I've got something interesting to tell you. A man by the name of Cocaine came in here looking for you, and baby, let me tell you. I ain't never wanted me a piece of chocolate so bad; I wanted to just bite into him."

Lexxy's heart immediately started racing as she thought about Cocaine, but she didn't want to seem too excited or too eager to see what he wanted. So she played it off as cool as possible.

"Oh, really? Well, what did he say?"

"Bitch, please don't try to act like you're not excited. That. Man. Is. Fine, do you hear me? I need you to quit trippin'. I told him you were in the hospital and what happened, he said the funniest thing afterwards."

"What's that?" Lexxy asked. She had no clue what Denise was going to say, but whatever it is made her body shake.

"He wanted to come and visit you, so I gave him the details on where you were. So hopefully he'll make it up there before you get discharged."

"YOU DID WHAT?" Lexxy shouted into the phone. Her cheeks felt like they would fall off they were so hot. She couldn't remember ever feeling this damn embarrassed in her life. Why would Denise do this to her? She and Lucky had only been broken up for a few days, and for all Denise knew, he could be a killer, rapist, or a serial killer rapist.

"Sure fucking did, bitch. I figured it would be nice to see you with someone who wasn't Lucky, and he seemed genuinely concerned, so…I don't know what to tell you. I guess you better prepare for the visit. Now I gotta go because I'm covering your shifts. I love you, bitch!" Denise slurred the word bitch so that it would stretch, and then she hung up.

Even if Cocaine did come see her, Wild Bill would have to meet him first, and that could be a doozy for most people. Wild Bill wasn't the most approachable person in the world, but something about Cocaine made her feel like he might not have as much trouble as the next person might have.

Lexxy continue lying in bed wondering if Cocaine was serious about coming to see her or not, and with the way she felt, she could only imagine how she looked. She didn't even want to check herself in the mirror that was in the bathroom, but she did because she didn't want to look dingy in front of him.

Why did she care so much? Why was she low-key checking for Cocaine? She was in for a world of change whether she knew it or not, and if Cocaine did come and visit....ooh wee, how was she supposed to react? Was she supposed to get upset? Because she wasn't. She couldn't find it in herself to genuinely be mad about him coming to see her. She just hoped when he did come that he would realize since she was in a hospital bed that she couldn't be worried about keeping up her appearance, that she needed to focus on getting better first, and then she could worry about her looks.

CHAPTER 7

A cold, sickening feeling came over Wild Bill as he stood guard at Lexxy's door. It was as if someone opened the door to the hospital and let a cold, chilly wind in. That was impossible because it was the middle of the summer, and the heat in July in Nashville could be fierce.

Nonetheless, the feeling caught Wild Bill's attention, and he had no choice but to look up. When he did, his eyes were met by a very tall, statuesque, man that dripped in hood royalty. He approached the registration desk, and the nurse pointed him in the direction of Wild Bill.

"Hey, my man, I'm looking for Lexxy, she in there?" Cocaine's smooth voice and nonchalant like demeanor had Wild Bill thrown off. Who was this nigga?

"Who are you?" Wild Bill asked with an attitude, and of course, that was his job. He loved Lexxy as if she was his own daughter, so he had to be on guard at all times, especially since this whole thing happened over a nigga.

"I'm Cocaine, and who might you be?"

Cocaine stood tall and looked Wild Bill right in the eyes, something he wasn't used to. People, men especially, usually looked away from him because he was crazy, and you know crazy when you see it, but the simple fact that Cocaine didn't seem even the slightest bit intimidated or worried about Wild Bill said a lot to him.

"Everybody calls me Wild Bill. You said you were here to see Lexxy?"

Wild Bill was confused. This young buck wasn't Lucky. Did Lexxy have another piece that the family didn't know about? At least, that's what Wild Bill was asking himself.

"Yeah, I met her a few days ago at work. I told her I wasn't gon' stop comin' her way until she gave me some time. I guess she thought I was playin'. When I got to the diner, her friend Denise told me she was up here because she was injured, so I bought her a little get well present."

Wild Bill looked into Cocaine's hands, and he didn't see anything, so he wondered what he could've possibly brought.

"Where it at then?"

Wild Bill wasn't a fool, and he would die lettin' somebody pull the wool over his niece's eyes, but there was something about Cocaine that Wild Bill liked, and he didn't feel like he had to pull the hardball stops on his ass.

Cocaine reached into his pocket and pulled out a small, blue box, with the word Zales across it. Wild Bill was a bit confused. Cocaine had just told him he met Lexxy a few days ago, and even though he was obviously trying to court Lexxy, what the hell was he doing with a jewelry box? Wild Bill was from the old school, and he was used to seeing shit like this back in the day when a cat would spring a ring, necklace, or bracelet up on you to show how serious they were about dating, but he hadn't seen anything like that in a very long time.

Cocaine opened the box, and inside was a watch, and not just any watch. The watch was diamond encrusted with a pink band for the wrist, and the clock face was small, trimmed in rose gold. As Wild Bill looked at the watch and noticed Cocaine's wrist was blinging, creating an even brighter glow that mixed with the watch still inside the box.

"Wow, young nigga, you sprung on my niece? Matchin' watches?"

Cocaine smiled and closed the box.

"Nah, I ain't sprung, I just know what I want, and I know how to get it. Ima show her how special I think she is and now that I know all of this happened over that lame ass boyfriend she was telling me she had. I wanna remind her that time is something you can never get back. Once it's gone that's it, and Ima make sure she remembers that, and yeah, it matches mine so she can realize her time would be better spent with me."

Wild Bill realized this little nigga was a smooth talker, but he could also sense his genuineness, and if this would help get that other idiot out of the picture, he was all for it. He wanted Lexxy to be happy, and even if she wasn't going to take this other dude seriously, at least she would know she had options.

"Cool. Well, I would say nah, you can't go in, but I got a good feelin' about you, so go ahead."

Cocaine shook hands with Wild Bill and flashed him his golden smile, and Wild Bill opened the door for him.

When Cocaine came in, Lexxy looked like she was

peacefully sleeping, and he didn't want to disturb her, but watching her sleep was one of the most beautiful things he'd ever seen. He didn't want to leave and miss it. Instead, he sat down in one of the chairs as quietly as possible and watched his Sleeping Beauty enjoy her rest.

An hour or so had passed by, and she was still asleep. Her chest was moving up and down, and she seemed so at peace. Cocaine couldn't believe the sweet girl he'd met at the diner that night would try to burn her house down over a nigga, but looks could be deceiving. He wondered what the nigga she was so proud to say was her man just the other night had done to her to set her off like that. This only confirmed what Cocaine already knew to be true, she needed a real nigga in her life. Not just any real nigga, but specifically him.

Cocaine decided he would leave the watch for her and write her a note letting her know exactly what it meant, but as he leaned over the table in her room, Lexxy rolled over and noticed he was there. She opened her eyes just a tiny bit, and even though she knew he was coming, she didn't know when so seeing him was still a surprise. She'd sat up for hours hoping he'd come when she was awake and looking as well as she could, but no, he had to come when she had drool coming all out of her mouth, her hair was nappy, and now that she had been sleep, her breath definitely stunk, and she probably was farting while she was asleep, but she hoped he hadn't been there that long.

"Hello, sunshine. How you feelin'?"

Cocaine placed his hand on the side of her face, and she couldn't help but smile.

"I'm ok. How are you? I'm surprised you came," she said, admitting the truth. Even though Denise said he was coming, the truth was that Cocaine didn't know her from a can of paint, so for him to come was mind-blowing to her.

"Oh, ya' girl put you up on game I see."

Lexxy tried hard not to read too deep into it. She couldn't understand why it was easy for a complete stranger to come visit her, and he didn't know her. Lucky's stupid ass hadn't figured it out yet....five years later.

"Yeah, she told me, but you didn't have to. Really, I'm ok. I should be going home tomorrow."

"Home? I hope not to the smoky hell that's your house now. Ya' bestie told me you can't go back there."

"At least not for now. There are a lot of things that will have to be done to it before it's livable again."

"Well, if you need a place, just let me know. I just bought a big house, you could have one half, and I could have the other, or we could stay on the same side. Whatever you like. What kind of color schemes you like, baby?"

Lexxy giggled and put her hand over her mouth to keep from showing her teeth that were probably turning yellow since she hadn't been able to brush them for the last few days.

"Cocaine, for all you know, I'm a serial killer."

"And for all you know, I'm one, but baby, you ain't no killer. I can smell the innocence on you."

Cocaine was right. Lexxy had never murdered anyone, but she wasn't as innocent as she seemed.

"So you say. So, how long have you been here? Hopefully not too long, I've been knocked out."

"Oh, I know. You were in here dead to the world, but I ain't mad at 'cha. It be like that sometimes. Besides, you looked good sleepin', like you were resting and at peace. I wouldn't mind seeing you like that every day."

Cocaine was laying it on thick, but he meant every word he said. He had truly never met anyone like Lexxy. Just from the few things he observed about her the night at the diner, and by the information her best friend was more than willing to tell to him when he stopped by the diner. Watching her sleep, he felt close to her, like he needed to know more about her and have her in his life. After he got revenge for his father's murder, he was going to want to settle down, and he was closer than ever to finally having everything he wanted. He wanted Lexxy to be a part of that. He would take it as slow as they needed to, as long as she understood the fact that he was a cold-blooded killer and street royalty. He was a king in his own right, and she would make for a fine ass queen.

"Cocaine, you've got to stop, you're making me blush," Lexxy giggled once more. She was enjoying being flirted with and made to feel special.

"Well, keep them red cheeks goin' Mrs. Clause, I got somethin' for you."

Lexxy's eyebrows flinched a bit when she heard those words. She wondered what he'd gotten for her, and she hoped he hadn't gone through too much trouble.

Cocaine took the box back out of his pocket and opened it for Lexxy. She was fixing her mouth to say no, but before she could, Cocaine was already taking it out of the box and putting it around her wrist.

"Perfect fit. You like it?"

Though Lexxy was used to having nice things, she was surprised to be receiving this type of gift from someone she didn't know.

"I-I love it, but I can't accept this."

"Of course you can, and I bought it specifically for you. Let me show you."

He pulled back the clasp that held the watch together and turned it over. On the inside of the band, it was inscribed with a little note.

"To the prettiest girl I know, Lexxy."

"I can't regift this, ma. I don't know anybody else named Lexxy, and I damn sure ain't spendin' no bread on nobody else but you. I keep tryna tell you, you gonna be mine."

As nice as that sounded, she didn't want to completely throw away her relationship with Lucky even though it seemed like it was pretty much in the trash. She loved him, and this...whatever she had growing between her and Cocaine, that feeling she got in her chest, the electricity between their touch, she wasn't sure was worth losing Lucky over. Sure, he left her, but that didn't mean that they were completely done. This wasn't the first time Lucky had tried some shit like this. Now she was regretting burning his things and almost losing her house. Her feelings were conflicted, and she didn't know what to do, and if the situation at hand wasn't already fucked up and crazy, it was about to get a lot worse.

Lexxy smiled and thanked Cocaine for her gift. She

stared at it, and then at him, and she realized he had a very similar watch. Cocaine was full of himself, and confidence radiated from his body like nothing she had ever seen.

"Our watches match? Wow," Lexxy said, astonished by the sight before her.

"Yeah, but that's just the beginning. You don't need a lot of nice things, you need a good man. A man to love you, spoil your heart and keep your mind occupied. You're too smart to be trippin' over a nigga who ain't ready to commit," Cocaine said bluntly, repeating what Denise had told him.

"Oh God, not you too. Let me guess, Denise told you?"

"She did—"

As Cocaine was talking, the door opened, and in walked a furious Lucky.

"What the hell you got goin' on in here, Lex? Who is this?" Lucky asked with his chest poked out like he was ready for a fight.

Lexxy wondered where the hell Wild Bill was and how he got in past him and then she wondered the same thing about Cocaine. Was Wild Bill slippin' today?

"Hey, Lucky. This is my friend, Cocaine. Cocaine, this is Lucky," Lexxy introduced the two men before her.

"Oh, this is the nigga that you burnt your house down over? Damn, really, bae?"

Cocaine gave Lucky a once-over, and he knew he wasn't about shit. He could see it all over him. A pretty dread-headed nigga who didn't know his ass from his face.

"Bae? What the fuck is he talkin' 'bout, bae?"

"Lucky, chill. Cocaine, I think you should go."

"Yeah, nigga, you need to move."

Cocaine looked Lucky in the eye, and he kept glancing from the floor to Cocaine like he was nervous.

"Yeah, BAE, I'm 'bout to get up out of here. I'ma come back tomorrow," Cocaine said as he brushed his fingers over Lexxy's watch. Lucky took notice of it, but instead of doing anything, he moved out the way so Cocaine could leave the room.

Lexxy was awestruck; she didn't know what to say or what to do. Lucky had left so angrily just a few days before, and now he was back in here acting like her man. The way she knew he would, she knew they weren't over. She just knew it.

The door slammed behind Cocaine, and Lucky was standing there looking like a scorned baby mama.

"Lexxy, the fuck was that? Who was that nigga? And what type of name is Cocaine? We been broke up a few days, and this the shit you do? Damn!"

Lucky took a seat in the chair Cocaine had just left, and Lexxy didn't feel like arguing. She wasn't going to, and she didn't owe Lucky an explanation. He chose to break up with her; it wasn't the other way around, so screw what he was talking about. He could be mad if he wanted to, but his words would hold no validity.

"He's a friend, but that doesn't matter, what do you want? Why are you here?"

Lucky reached over the bed railing and grabbed Lexxy's hand and kissed it. He looked deep into her eyes, hoping to pull her soul out. He searched for the words to say and realized how he could nip all of this in the bud. He loved Lexxy, and he didn't want to lose her, especially not to the likes of a nigga like Cocaine. Lucky felt like Cocaine coming into the picture changed things, and he'd be damned if he lost his woman to a hood nigga. Lucky was a punk at heart, he'd never even been in a real fight in his entire life, but this was the only way he could think to prove to Lexxy that he didn't want to lose her.

"I came back because you're my woman, and I overreacted. I wanted to apologize; I also wanted to tell you that I just wanna be with you. However I have to be so we can make this work. I don't wanna lose you, baby. I'm sorry for exploding on you a few days ago. I really am. I was just so fuckin' mad. Like, you too smart to be doin' stupid shit like that, baby, but we don't even gotta talk about that. I do want you to move in, especially now with the house being unlivable. I wanna be the one to take care of you, the one that you can depend on. I don't want you lookin' anywhere else for help because I'm all you need, baby. You're mine, and I'm yours. It's a forever type of thing," Lucky said. He didn't want to lose Lexxy because he loved her, but he also knew no other woman would want to deal with his ass. So he had to hurry up and get it together before he missed out on his chance at true love.

The bright shining diamonds glistened against Lexxy's wrist as Lucky spoke to her. For some reason, she felt torn. She wanted to be with Lucky, but would she be making a mistake by taking him back? She couldn't say for sure, but at least she knew Lucky, and she knew what being with him was like. Cocaine, though he appeared to be nice, wasn't where her heart was, but she couldn't get him out of her mind. However, Lucky admitting he wanted to be with her and was ready to commit awoke something inside of her that she thought died the night he pulled the house key stunt. If he was finally ready, she would take him back because that was all she wanted anyway.

She thought about her words carefully before saying them, not wanting to damage or ruin the moment. She spoke softly, but firmly.

"Lucky, you know I love you. I always have, and I always will. All I've ever wanted was for us to be happy and in love, and if you're serious then I want to get back together. I can't take another backwards moment. I don't want to keep moving through time without certainty of what's going on between us. We need to be on the same page."

Lucky nodded his head and leaned down, kissing her passionately on the lips. The vibrations she thought she could no longer feel for Lucky were back like they never left.

"All I want is you, baby. I want you, us, and eventually, I want us to be a family."

At the sound of the word family, Lexxy's eyes began watering. That was all she wanted. To grow old with her man, and they be madly in love with one another and start a family that could continue on her family's lineage.

"I love you, Lucky."

"I love you too, baby. Now listen, I'm about to go home and get the stuff ready for you to come home since you should be getting discharged tomorrow. I want you to be comfortable, so I'ma go out and get a few things for you. I'll be here to get you in the afternoon since that's when the doctor said you'd probably be released."

Lexxy nodded her head, and a smile crept across her lips. She and Lucky were about to be living together and finally be TRULY committed to one another.

Lucky walked out the door, and Wild Bill peaked his head inside. Lexxy was shocked to see him since he'd done a little disappearing act before.

"Unc, where the hell you been at?" Lexxy asked as she started laughing.

"Shit, I went to the bathroom for a second. I come back, and you got both ya' niggas visitin'? I can dig it, niece, be careful, somebody's goin' end up with their heart broken. I hope it's that Lucky nigga. He's weak, but that Cocaine, he's somethin' else. I wonder who his people are."

Lexxy hadn't asked, and until that moment, she hadn't even thought about it. Now she wondered where he came from and how ironic it was that he appeared during a stressful, strange time between her and her boyfriend. She knew she couldn't keep him around, so tomorrow she'd have to return the watch and let him know that she and Lucky were back together, and she planned on making that work at all costs.

The next morning, Lexxy was finally ready to go home, well to her new home with Lucky. He'd been texting her all night, and she fell asleep talking to him. Something they hadn't done in a very long time. When they first met, they used to spend their nights talking and laughing, just getting to know one another. It had been such a long time since she was able to truly enjoy her man. It was like the beginning of their relationship all over again.

Lexxy was able to get up out of the bed and move on her own, and that's exactly what she was doing. Wild Bill had called Denise and asked her to bring Lexxy some things so she could look presentable when she left. When she showed up that morning, she had an attitude because she took Lucky back. But Lexxy was on cloud nine, and nobody was going to bring her down, not even her best friend, who though she was just trying to protect her, was a buzz kill. She was in love with Lucky, and only she could say when it was time to stop giving that nigga chances. She'd give him as many as her heart could take, and only she could say when she'd had enough, period.

Lexxy looked at herself in the mirror, and she was somewhat dirty from the ashes that sprinkled over her in the house, or at least her hair was. She wanted to wash it, but she wasn't sure if she had the strength or energy to stand up and do it herself. So she wet the comb Denise brought her and ran it through her thick hair, hoping it would bring some type of curl back to it, and it did immediately. She took out the body wash and washcloth the hospital gave her, and she started the shower. She couldn't wait to wash her body because she felt filthy, and for the last few days, she'd been giving herself hoe baths out of a small container. So she couldn't wait to let the warm water run over her body.

She stepped out of the blue, polka-dotted hospital gown and got into the shower. The hot water against her body felt damn near orgasmic. She had waited way too long to get in the shower, not that she wanted to because if it was up to her, she would've been in here by now, but the doctors wouldn't let her, and they said she needed to wait. Now that she was actually in here, she couldn't even understand how she was able to lay up for the last few days like this, and she was thankful that she was going to school to be a doctor so she could help her patients through tough times like this. She hoped she never lost a patient or came across something she couldn't fix. She knew that was unrealistic, there just wasn't an answer or a cure to everything, but she would do everything she could and exhaust all options when that time came if she ever graduated. While she was laid up the last few days, she should've been studying, but instead, she was worried about some boy.

Lexxy poured the Tahitian Caress soap onto the washcloth and began scrubbing her body. While she was in a peaceful, tranquil place in her mind, she heard the door open. Her eyes hadn't been open until that moment, but she had to open them to see who had come in her room. Wild Bill was outside, so he should've announced whoever was coming in. Boy, he had been slipping on his job.

Lexxy pulled the shower curtain back and looked into the room, and there was Cocaine, sitting in the seat beside the bed. He wore a black button-down with gray joggers and black Huaraches. She wondered where he was going dressed like that, but to her surprise, he looked handsome. She wasn't used to anyone wearing a dress shirt and kind of casual pants and looking that good. She needed to quickly push that thought out of her mind because she had a man, and she was about to have to break the news to Cocaine again that she wasn't interested. She now realized taking the watch from Cocaine was a mistake, but in the moment, it didn't seem like it. She was just so happy to have some attention from a man. That she didn't necessarily care who it came from. Now, her main problem was worrying if Lucky came in while she was in the shower while Cocaine was in the room as well. He told her he'd be back today, but she hoped she'd be gone by the time he got there, so she'd miss him altogether.

"I'll be right out, give me a second!" Lexxy called from the shower. She was glad she thought to bring her clothes in the bathroom with her. She couldn't see herself getting dressed in a wide-open room like that, so she remembered to bring them in there with her, and now that Cocaine was there, she was more than glad. She would've been humiliated if he would've seen her naked, and she knew he would've never let her live it down anyway.

Lexxy finished washing up and got out the shower, quickly trying to dress in case Lucky just happened to show up, and she needed to break the truth to Cocaine quickly. Lexxy got dressed in record speed, barely drying her body off, and then she slipped on the flip-flops Denise had brought her, and she came out of the bathroom.

Cocaine's face lit up as soon as he saw her which of course caused her to smile, spreading that contagious infatuation to her.

"It's good to see you back on two feet, baby. You look good," Cocaine said as he walked to her. She quickly stuck her hands out, and her hands touched his chest. She could feel every ripple in his pecks, and she wondered how often he worked out because clearly, he wasn't skipping any days.

"Listen Cocaine; I can't see you anymore. I mean, like ever again, and I have to give you back the watch. It was a beautiful present and an even sweeter gesture, but Lucky and I are back together. I don't want to send him or you the wrong message by accepting such a large gift."

As Lexxy spoke, she kept her hands on his chest, and she could feel his heart beating. His heartrate began to pick up as he continued listening to her talk. Had Lexxy been some bum bitch, he would've dismissed himself, but he couldn't do that with her. He would never disrespect Lexxy, even though she was telling him to step off. Cocaine was persistent, and he didn't give a damn about

Lucky. He fucked up once, and he would fuck up again, and when he did, Cocaine would be there to sweep Lexxy back off her feet.

"Yo', I feel you wanna be faithful to your man, and you don't even know how much I appreciate that. It lets me know when you come home with me that I can trust you and count on you, so I'm not even trippin'. I'm not takin' that watch back, baby. It's yours, keep it. You don't even ever have to wear it. I just want you to have it. I can't take it back no damn way, and a nigga got a soft spot for you. Seein' that watch every day wouldn't do nothin' but break me down. You want me to be cryin' and shit?" he asked as he put his fingers underneath her chin and made her look him in the eye.

Lexxy was bashful, but it had become much more than that. She was seeing something in Cocaine, something she'd seen in Lucky, and that scared her. She was getting too close to the situation, and she had to separate herself before it was too late.

She removed her hands and took a step back from him. Her pouty lips plumped with sadness as she looked at him once more.

"Cocaine, I'm serious. We can't be friends, we can't talk, none of that. I don't want Lucky thinking I'm unfaithful."

"You already have been, baby, the moment you looked into my eyes and tried to lie to yourself about how you feel, but it's cool. I swear I understand, and I ain't tryna apply no pressure to you, baby. I just want what's best for you, truly."

He rubbed his hand across her smooth face, and

instead of kissing her on the cheek like he wanted to, he just walked away.

"I really just wanted to check on you. I'm glad you're feelin' better, ma."

Cocaine walked out of the room, and Lexxy felt guilty. Not because she told him to leave, but because she felt a tinge of regret for saying it.

She sat down on her bed and thought about the things that had taken place that day already. She and Denise had gotten into the same argument they always did when it came to Lucky. She had to tell Cocaine to step off, and to her surprise, he did. How was something like that even possible? She didn't know. He was so persistent, and he was giving up on her. Why did she even care so much?

Her thoughts of Cocaine were of course interrupted by Lucky walking through the door with a large bouquet of Tulips, her favorite flower.

"Hello, beautiful. You ready to go home?" Lucky asked as the nurse walked in behind him with Lexxy's discharge papers. Although she was ready to go home, and she was smiling on the outside, she couldn't deny the sad feeling she felt in her heart for cutting off Cocaine, but she had to do it, right? Had she made the right decision?...

Lexxy made it home, and even though she'd been to Lucky's house many times, it was nothing like actually calling this her place to live as well. As soon as she walked through the door, she instantly began thinking of how she needed to change her mailing address for her bills and billing information. She couldn't believe this was finally happening. It was almost surreal, and the way Lucky was acting, it was almost brand new for Lexxy. Since he'd picked her up, he'd practically been babying her. Lexxy didn't want to go directly home when she left the hospital. They'd been to get ice cream, eat, went to the park to let Lexxy stretch her legs, and now, they were finally home after a full day. Normally, Lucky would complain about having to do all of this driving, but not today. Today, he was being the perfect gentleman and a yes man. Whatever Lexxy wanted, he was giving it to her just to keep her happy. After all, that's what you did when you loved someone.

As Lexxy looked around the house, she realized everything around her was different. Lucky had done some decorating and changed a few things, and they were all to her liking. When she'd first seen this place three years ago, she told him there were a few adjustments he should make, and now to see him make them in just twenty-four hours, she couldn't believe it.

His walls were painted a very dark brown; she'd suggested changing them to a nude color to bring more light into the house. They weren't vampires. He'd upgraded his lamps from the small, table lights, to full scale, long, chic lamps, and she even noticed they were the energy saving light bulbs. Lucky often complained about his light bill, and Lexxy told him how to keep his light bill down a little bit, and he was finally listening. If this was a preview of what she had to look forward to, she liked it a lot.

"You ok, baby?" he asked as he took her stuff into the house and helped her walk up the stairs.

"Go slow, I don't want you falling," Lucky said genuinely. He was trying his best to do everything to make her happy and show her he could be the guy she met before. Not someone who wasn't serious about her or who didn't deserve her, like Cocaine. Since seeing him in Lexxy's room, he was all that Lucky could think about. He realized he almost lost his woman, and he wasn't going to have that. So no matter what he had to do, he was willing to do it.

Lexxy came up the stairs, and the smell of lavender instantly hit her nose.

"Candles?" she asked.

"Nah, the house would've been done burned down by now, no pun intended or shade. I bought those flower things you told me to get to make the room smell better and not so musty. I guess it's pretty strong if you can smell it from the hallway."

Lexxy smirked and threw her arms around Lucky's neck. He didn't know it, but he was probably about to get some pussy tonight. If Lexxy could stay awake long enough to make it happen. Since she had a full day, and she had antibiotics and pain meds, she didn't want to make any promises, especially because she was already tired.

"I love you, Lucky."

"I love you too, baby, now come on. Let's get you in the room so you can get some rest, ok?"

Lexxy agreed. She would normally put up a fight about getting in the bed before six p.m. but she couldn't this time, no way, no how was that going to happen tonight. She wanted the dick, but her body craved sleep, so she'd be giving into it more than likely as soon as she got into the bed. When she opened the door to their room, even thinking those words made her feel good, she gasped in shock. The room had completely transformed since the last time she was here. The red and black bedsheets that were from Walmart had been thrown out, and now the bed was white and black with the matching pillowcases, something she'd begged Lucky to do, to at least let the pillowcases on the bed match, and now they were. The room was clean, livable even, which was rare. Normally, when Lexxy was here, she found herself spending most of her time cleaning than actually spending time with him. The closet door was open, organized, and even had some of her clothes inside, but they had the price tags still on them.

"Lucky, you didn't? You bought me my clothes, like the same ones?"

"Yep. I wanted you to feel as at home and as comfortable as you possibly could, and that's not it either. Go on in the bathroom."

Lucky licked his top row of teeth anticipating how she was going to react to what was inside.

Lexxy hobbled over to the bathroom and cut the light on. On the sink was the $350 toothbrush kit that had been on back order for almost a year, so she didn't understand how he was able to get one in just a day.

"Lucky, how the hell did you have time for all this shit and the toothbrush? How was that even possible?"

He came into the bathroom and picked her up, placing her on the sink and getting between her legs. He wrapped his arms around her waist and rubbed one hand around the back of her head.

"It's amazing the shit you can do when you really wanna do it. I just started thinking about what would make you happy and what I could do to make you comfortable. I just started shopping, spending money on shit that I remembered you mentioning, and the toothbrush, I got lucky. I passed a dentist's office, and I went straight inside and asked to just buy it straight out. I had no shame."

Lexxy giggled and pulled at Lucky's dreads. They were up in a bun like always. She wanted to feel his hair, so she took the bun down and ran her fingers through the back of it, massaging his scalp, and then she kissed him. She kissed him for all he had done and all he was going to do. She was surprised by the sweet gestures and efforts he made.

"I'ma go get the bed ready for you, wait here," he said as he pulled away from her.

After a few minutes, Lexxy started to feel even more tired than she had before. She was ready to go to bed, so she hopped off the counter, ignoring Lucky's words. When she got back into the room from the connected bathroom, there was a small box on the bed, the same box she'd gotten at the restaurant just days before.

"You don't have to regive me the key like this. It's cool, you can just hand it to me, baby," Lexxy said, unamused, but she tried not to let it show. This was just reminding her of how she wasn't able to seal the deal with her own man.

"How do you know it's a key?" Lucky asked as he took off his shirt and slid out of his pants. His body looked like it had wax all over it he was so shiny.

Lexxy cut her eyes at him. This couldn't be what she hoped it was. She'd gotten her hopes up before, and she wasn't going to do it again. She reached for the box and opened it, and she looked up with tears in her eyes.

"Lucky....are you sure?" she asked as she looked at Lucky who was now on one knee right in front of her.

"Baby, I did this wrong the first time, and I'm so sorry. I love you, and I never realized it before, but I'm afraid to lose you. You're the best thing that's ever happened to me, so if you'll have me, I want you to be my wife."

Lexxy's hands flew to her mouth, and she fell to the bed. Her legs had finally given out on her. But even as she fell, she still held the ring tightly in her hand as if she was Gollum from Lord of the Rings.

Lucky laughed as she collapsed on the bed, and he climbed on top of her, his dick rock hard, and his heart beating out of his chest. He leaned down over her and started pecking her on the neck, and then the cheek, and then on her face, and she laughed the entire time. She hadn't been this happy ever.

Lexxy handed Lucky the ring, and he slid it on her ring finger. He was proud of himself. In just a day's time, he'd been able to temporarily fix all of their problems. If he would've done this way before now, the house incident would've never happened.

Looking at her ring, Lexxy thought about her watch, and how they were both making bold statements. It wasn't a choice that was up for debate. She'd chosen Lucky, and that was the end of it.

As she admired her new jewelry, Lucky got off of her, and it snapped her back into reality. She'd felt his hard dick and thought she was about to get some to celebrate this momentous occasion.

She looked at Lucky and all but started whining.

"Uhn-uhn, not tonight. You had a long day. Get you some rest, baby, and I promise I'll give you some dick tomorrow. Now be good for daddy," he said as he got in the bed on the other side.

Lexxy exhaled, and then she pulled off her clothes with his help, and she got in beside him.

Though Lexxy was tired, she was so excited, and she couldn't wait to tell anyone who would listen about her and Lucky's engagement. She crawled into his arms, and as the minutes passed by, she fell asleep, feeling like that happily ever after was afoot.

CHAPTER 9

A few weeks later, Lexxy was feeling one hundred percent better, and she couldn't have been in a better place with Lucky. She was happy, and everything she wanted was finally coming true, talk about a fairy tale romance. The house that was once Lucky's alone was now hers as well, and she loved coming home.

Lexxy has been so happy, she was able to relax long enough to study for her big exam, and she actually passed, which meant she'd be graduating soon. She would be able to go to work at the hospital full time the way she wanted, and everything would be all good.

Throughout her undergrad years, she had done internships and walk along with fellow doctors, but she didn't want a position full time until she completed college because she didn't want to be a floater, nor did she want to follow behind another doctor. She wanted her own shit so she could eventually open a black-owned practice. She believed in her black culture, and she wanted to help promote black power in her community by being a part of it. If you were tired of seeing something the same way, you had to be the change you wanted to see, and that was Lexxy's ultimate goal.

Since Lexxy had moved in with Lucky, he'd taken

more shifts at work so she wouldn't have to rush back to work so soon. Even though she did go to work sometimes, she didn't take nearly as many shifts as she did before because Lucky made it clear that he wanted to take care of her and she didn't need to stress herself out. Their relationship had changed and grown so much in such a small amount of time. Lexxy felt like the things she'd said to Lucky were finally getting across to him, and that he was taking their relationship more seriously, but for Lucky, it was a different story.

At first, him coming home to Lexxy was everything he wanted. He loved waking up to her and not needing to know her schedule because he knew exactly where she would be when he got back. He didn't have to check in with her as much, and he had a little more freedom throughout the day with less pressure of having to talk to her all day on the phone or text her all day because she was right there in his house. That was the main thing he loved, but those things weren't enough to keep him from losing his mind honestly.

Lucky never saw himself getting married or settling down. He always thought he and Lexxy would be together and just be happy, but then she started pressuring him, and he had to step up to the plate, or he would lose her. But now, her being there every day changing shit, touching stuff, going through his things, made him insane! He didn't want to yell at her and tell her to stop, but he wanted things to go back to how they were before. Lexxy was spoiled, and he couldn't rip the comfort she felt away from her, not without potentially losing her for good.

Every day after work though Lucky was taking extra shifts. He often found himself at a bar, drinking beer, drowning his self in sorrows for not wanting to grow up. Any man would be lucky to even get close to Lexxy, and he knew that. But for whatever reason, he couldn't seem to get that settle down mentality to stick. Lucky had never cheated on Lexxy, and he never would, but that didn't mean he wanted to be tied down to where he couldn't get a lil' snack if he really wanted to. This shit had him fucked up, and though he'd been putting on a brave face, today, he was finally about to drop his act. He couldn't fake the funk anymore or pretend he was completely happy because he was honestly spoiled and used to having things his way. Now they weren't going his way, so he was torn between himself and Lexxy.

Instead of stopping at the bar after work, he decided to go straight home and just go to bed. It was already late since he stayed a few hours past his normal work time, so he figured he'd go home, eat, and then pass out.

When he got into the house, Lexxy had dinner on the table, and she was sitting at the table, patiently waiting for him to join her.

"Hi, baby, how was your day?"

"Cool," Lucky said, hoping this wouldn't make Lexxy keep talking. Since she'd made dinner, he felt like he had to sit down and eat it now. He couldn't just let the food go to waste, especially since he was the one who bought it.

He took off his shoes and put them by the door, and then he came and sat down next to her. Lexxy could feel something was bothering him, but she wanted to ask in a way that wouldn't annoy him because she knew how he could be.

Lucky, you sure you ok? You're probably tired from working all day." Lexxy's tone was small and sweet. She didn't want to add to the tension that was already present between the two.

"I'm good. Why you ain't eat already? You didn't have to wait for me."

Lexxy was amused but also confused by his statement. He was right, she didn't have to wait for him, but if she didn't, he would bitch. He always complained whenever she cooked a meal and didn't wait for him to get home to eat it. He hated eating at the large kitchen table alone.

"Well, you said you didn't like to—"

"It don't matter, don't worry about it," Lucky snapped at Lexxy.

She didn't know what his problem was and why he was bitching at her. He had a real issue, and she wanted to know what it was. Since she'd been living there, she thought Lucky was happy, and now that he was being snappy. She wondered if her presence was bothering him. He'd been making little remarks that he said were jokes, but she knew they had some underlying truth. Like when she did laundry and folded the clothes as soon as they came from the dryer, he'd always say, 'Guess you can't just let them clothes sit in the basket. They goin' go in the drawer hot and be all stiff when I gotta put 'em on,' or 'I guess the dishwasher don't get the dishes clean enough since you always wash them in the sink. Me puttin' 'em in the dishwasher ain't good enough."

At first, Lexxy thought it was funny, but every day, it wasn't, but she figured they just needed to get used to the living arrangements. Before ,she could just go home if they got into it, and so could he, but now, they lived together. So if they got into it, there was nowhere for either of them to go, and there was no getting away from one another,which was why ultimately they both tried to avoid a fight from happening because they knew exactly what could happen because of it.

Lexxy chose not to pester him anymore about what the problem was even though she desperately wanted to know what was bothering him. She decided to sit there and eat her food, and if he wanted to tell her, then he would.

An hour later, they were done eating and had hardly said a word to one another. Lexxy cleaned off the table, washed the dishes, and put them in the dish rack to dry. Lucky had gone upstairs to take a shower, but he didn't even say thank you, which was weird and uncommon, but Lexxy didn't want to press the issue.

Since she'd had her piro moment, sex for the two of them had been difficult. She was embarrassed by her burns and bruises, even though they weren't too big or anything that she should be ashamed of, but she was, so she didn't want to get completely naked in front of him. She thought maybe that was where another part of their problems came from, so tonight, she was going to pull out the extra freak in her and turn the heat all the way up for Lucky. Considering she didn't want him to leave her for not sexually satisfying him, or worse, cheat on her. If he did, she would definitely have him killed. Wild Bill would be hearing from her and coming to see Lucky if that was the case. Lexxy could tolerate a lot, but being cheated on was not one of them.

Lucky had just gotten out of the shower and was on the bed on his phone. Something was troubling him on the screen. Lexxy could tell by the way his face was turned up like someone just threw a cat at his face. Lexxy plopped down on the bed and started rubbing his back.

"What's going on, baby? What's the matter?"

"Damn, Lexxy, I said I'm cool. Why you keep asking me? You want it to be something wrong?"

"Why would I want there to be something wrong? I just know you, and I know when something is bothering you, I'm sorry for asking."

"Yeah, but I'm good, so don't ask me again!" Lucky yelled as he yanked away from her and went into the bathroom and slammed the door behind him.

Lexxy began replaying the events of the day in her mind once more trying to figure out what she could have done to him to make him act this way. Had she truly pissed him off, was she trippin'? Was he just trippin'?

Lexxy was trying to let it go, but now seeing his face as he looked at his phone, she knew something was wrong. There was no better way than to relax him than by giving him some of her pussy. He always said it made him relax and calm down, so she was going to give it to him, also because she was horny, and she wanted to feel her man.

Lexxy opened the bathroom door and immediately dropped to her knees. She started yanking on his pants aggressively, something she had done in the past that he truly enjoyed, but he recoiled when she touched him. He literally jumped away from her.

Lexxy stood up and was surprised, but she was also hurt. She'd never been pushed away by him, what was really going on?

"Not tonight, baby. I had a hard day. Maybe tomorrow."

Did he just give her the male equivalent of "I got a headache?"

Lexxy watched Lucky put his phone into his pocket and then climb into bed. He had on his pajamas, so he was bed ready. But now, Lexxy wouldn't be able to rest. She had been denied, Lucky had an attitude, and nothing seemed to be going right all of a sudden. Was her dream of wanting to be together becoming too much for Lucky? She didn't know, but she wished he'd just tell her what the deal was.

Even though she wasn't tired, Lexxy crawled into bed and snuggled up next to Lucky. Wanting to feel his strong body and his warmth, but he wasn't having that tonight. He turned away from her almost as soon as she got in bed and pulled the covers over his body. He didn't turn the light out, which meant she'd have to do it herself, but she was already in bed and becoming very irritable. Lucky was on some other shit, and Lexxy just hoped she found out what it was before it was too late.

She got out of bed, cut the lights off, and climbed back into bed with an already sleeping Lucky.

Since leaving the hospital and practically being denied, Cocaine had been plotting on his target, preparing to take his ass out. Since he was living just a few houses down, it was easy to watch him and even easier to come up with a plan of how to handle his opponent. He was going to kill him the exact same way he killed his father, with a few modifications. He was going to cut the gorilla tattoo off his face because he was unworthy of wearing it. He didn't deserve to be a part of the gang that was founded on hope, truth, and the desire to win against poverty.

Cocaine wished he knew then who all his father had done business with so he would know exactly who this man was, but he figured it was probably for the best because he was going to kill anyone involved, and he wasn't just thinking the main person involved, he was taking out full bloodlines, and that was how it was going to be. So if the other people were smart, they wouldn't be caught dead getting involved because it was going to go all the way south.

The summer night air was warm, but not too hot; perfect for a murder. This wouldn't be the first time Cocaine had to kill someone, and strangely enough, he had a specific time he loved to get rid of someone, and it was this type of weather. The rain made him want to relax, but the summertime gave him energy, and it made him want to get things done. He was about to have that chance, to get rid of the man who took everything from him.

Normally, Cocaine liked to do his dirty work far away so it could never lead back to him, but nobody even knew who he was, so he didn't mind taking care of this problem head-on. He was going to handle this nigga on his own, and do it well.

As he left his house, Cocaine made sure he had everything he would need to get the job done. He had his filleting knife he was going to use to fillet the nigga's face, his favorite gun that he affectionately nicknamed Baby… she had seen him through some tough situations, and he had a cleanup crew one of his friends back home had told him about on standby. The only thing left to figure out was how he was going to penetrate what was supposed to be an "impenetrable" fortress.

Cocaine knew taking his car would only draw more attention, and if the neighborhood was set up the way he thought it was from his observation, he would be able to climb over his fence and sneak in through the back, but what would be waiting on the other side of the fence was what bothered Cocaine. He didn't care about dying in battle, but he was going to take the gorilla faced man with him, period.

He approached the fence with his bag, ready to handle business, but he needed to see what he was dealing with first. He'd made it into the other person's backyard without anyone noticing him, so he was feeling confident and ready to get this shit over with, but he was smart. He wasn't going to throw himself into the lion's den without knowing what he was going into. He threw his bag over the fence just to see if someone would shoot, or if someone would pop out. He threw the bag over the fence, and after twenty minutes of nothing happening, he figured it was safe.

Cocaine climbed over the large fence, landing on his feet, and he scooted with his back faced toward the fence alongside it, so he could still watch what was going on around him.

As he got closer to the house, he noticed movement. It was just after nine p.m, and after days of following him around and studying his schedule, he knew that he was usually in the upstairs part of his home. He had seen him many nights when he snuck into his neighbor's house to watch him from across the street. He'd been able to watch him for a week straight without them knowing anyone had been in their home, which was also very strange to Cocaine. From what he could tell, the gorilla man didn't have any children and no wife, but many henchmen who surrounded his home and were on the inside, but for some reason, he was upstairs tonight, and there were only three henchmen that he could see.

Cocaine continued to creep along the side of the house, and by the time he got into the shadow of the yard, there were people coming out of the house, so he started letting off Baby. He didn't want to shoot to kill; he just wanted to injure. He also needed to take out his men too, so he pulled out Baby's big sister, Pelican, nicknamed after the extended clip onthe end, and started firing both guns.

The henchman ducked and rolled on top of their boss, trying to shield him from getting wounded. Some of the men were firing their guns back and trying to run in the direction the shots were coming from to take the shooter out, but they were idiots if they thought Cocaine would be taken out. His thirst for revenge is part of what kept him alive. He would do everything in his power to make sure he took his father's killer to hell with him.

The men got closer to Cocaine, so he took off running, which made him lose sight of his original target. It was no way he was going to be able to defend himself against all of them, and he hated to run, but it was the only way he would live to fight another day. He grabbed his bag and jumped back over the fence. The henchmen were too big to be running after him, so he wasn't worried about that. Cocaine was in amazing shape; he trained every day, so him getting away was nothing, but it only put him further behind.

As he ran back to his house, taking the back way he'd made for himself, his thoughts quickly fell upon Lexxy, and how he wanted to hurry up and get this shit over with so, he could settle down with his life. He didn't care shit about Lucky. He'd kill the nigga if he had to so that he could have what he wanted. He enjoyed the challenge and the fact that Lexxy thought he wasn't going to have her amused him.

When Cocaine got back to his house, he threw his bag down in the living room and went upstairs to text the cleaning crew to let them know tonight wouldn't be happening so they just wouldn't be waiting around for him to call. He knew they had other shit to do; those niggas stayed busy.

He took out his phone and started to text them when a text came in on his phone from an unknown number.

Although he didn't know who it was, he decided to go ahead and open it up. He didn't know that many people with a (615) area code number, so he thought maybe this person had the wrong number.

As he read the message, he realized it could only be one person...Denise. What did she want with Cocaine?

Reading the message, Cocaine smiled and licked his juicy brown lips. Shit was about to get real interesting.

CHAPTER 11

Since moving out of Lucky's place, and she did that immediately after she got back home, she had gone to stay with Denise. Something she reminded her she should have done from the beginning, but she didn't want to. Lexxy wanted to be with her man, and it all be good. She wanted to know what that was like, to experience happiness in her relationship and not have to worry about the rest. She couldn't believe how quickly this had gone south. She was happy because if this would have never happened, Lexxy would've stayed in that sad relationship. She would have either wound up dumped or miserable forever, and neither of those options were really in her favor.

The day had finally come for Lexxy to graduate, and it was a bittersweet day. She thought that she'd be more excited, or that the event would be more climactic, but she couldn't seem to get excited about it, nor did she feel like she was doing anything special. Sure, she'd worked all this time for this, but without Lucky, it almost seemed like it wasn't worth it. She hadn't cried, and she hadn't told Denise the details, but her best friend knew her. She knew when something wasn't right, and the fact of the matter was she felt like trash. She felt like Lucky used her for some reason, and he didn't even care or understand what he did.

Lexxy's graduation day was not all it was cracked up to be. This day was supposed to be special, but it was turning out to be anything but that. Lexxy was dressed and ready to go, and even with her makeup, her wallet, keys, cap, and gown, something still seemed as though it were missing as if she weren't whole.

Lexxy couldn't say that she missed Lucky, not yet anyway. Not with the way he'd been acting, but what she could say was that she was lonely. She missed having that attention from her man, well, the man she was now sharing with another woman.

"Bitch, you better perk up! It's time to go," Denise yelled as they were leaving the house. Lexxy couldn't believe she had to move in with Denise until her new place was ready. She wasn't going home, even though that was always an option. Lexxy was right back at square one, where she was when she started the fire.

Lexxy put on her best smile and pretended like she was happy, but Denise knew her, and she knew she was upset. As they walked to the car, Denise tried cracking jokes and making her laugh, but Lexxy was not up for it. She would giggle a little bit, but as far as full-blown laughter, that was not happening, and Denise should've known it.

When they got in the car, Denise couldn't take it anymore. She would do anything for her best friend's special day not to be ruined. So she turned on some trap music to see if that would get her in the spirit. She turned on Yung Dolph's song "Foreva" blasting it through the speakers as they rolled down the highway.

Lexxy's father was out of town, and so was her mother, so the only person who would be able to go was Wild Bill, which even though that was great, it made her feel lonely. Her father had always put his work in front of her, and that hurt. That was not something she wanted to feel, or that any child, no matter how old they were, should have to feel. For once, she just wanted to be at the top of someone's list, a priority and not an option.

By the time they got to the graduation, and Denise had played every trap song on her musical playlist, Lexxy was somewhat ready to walk across the stage, but she wasn't feeling excited. The pride she felt for making this accomplishment was now gone. She didn't care about the graduation or any of the people around her because she actually hated them, and they irritated her.

Her attitude didn't stop Denise from taking pictures of her, making her do crazy poses, and posting her pictures on Instagram. She was proud of her best friend and wanted nothing but the best for her. She saw all the shit she went through with Lucky, and she just wanted her to be happy, to smile again like she had before. When Lexxy went across that stage, Denise jumped up and started Milly Rocking.

Lexxy smiled and laughed as she put the tassle on the other side of her head, and when she got to the end of the stage, she did a mini Milly, letting her bestie know she received the dance and she was trying to loosen up.

When Lexxy got off the stage, she ran out into the crowd and wrapped her arms around Wild Bill who had tears in his eyes. She didn't see him before the graduation started, so she assumed he was going to miss it and probably take her out sometime later, but he didn't miss it. He made it just in time to see her walk across the stage.

"Uncle!" Lexxy said as she threw herself into his arms like a small child or a spider monkey.

"I'm so proud of you! Look at you, Doctor Lexxy."

"Stop, Unc! Thank you for coming," Lexxy said sincerely. She was genuinely happy that he was able to make it. Well that he was willing to sacrifice whatever he had going on that day to make it.

"I wouldn't miss this for the world, baby girl. Now, what do you ladies have planned for the evening? I figured I could come and do security for you so I can make sure you'll be safe. I know how y'all like to party. I don't wanna be worried abou—"

"No need to worry, Wild Bill. I'm here, I can look after the girls," Cocaine said as he walked right into their conversation.

Lexxy hadn't seen Cocaine in quite a while, so seeing him here like this was overwhelming. He was dressed in a blue and white button down, with the Polo Khakis, and Clark loafers. He'd come out to somewhat impress.

"Hello, beautiful, congratulations," he said as he bent down and kissed Lexxy's hand.

"Uhm…thank you. What are you doing here? How did you know?"

"Denise told me. I gave her my number to give to you that day I came to the diner. She texted me and let me know you'd be here, I didn't wanna miss this. I told you, baby, you're gonna be mine one day."

As soon as Cocaine said that, she instantly regretted the one thing she told herself not to do before she left the house. Which was not to wear this watch. She couldn't avoid it though, and it just so happened to look good with the dress she had on underneath her gown. Was this thing like some sort of magnet? Was she able to draw him near just by wearing it?

"Well, I appreciate you for coming, but you didn't have to."

"Yes, I did. This was a major accomplishment for you, baby. I wasn't goin' miss it, so be cool and let me come out with y'all tonight so I can keep up with you. I don't wanna have to kill nobody."

Wild Bill looked up and into his eyes, and he hadn't seen it before, but now he saw the cold killer that lived behind his eyes. He knew he'd protect Lexxy at all costs.

"Yeah baby, you know what, y'all need a young buck out wit' ya, not my old ass. Why don't you go ahead and let Cocaine take you, and I'll take you out to lunch sometime soon, ok, baby?"

Lexxy wanted to protest, but she couldn't. Denise had her arm in a choke grip making her do what Cocaine was telling her to do. After a few minutes of silence and awkward faces, and Denise pinching the shit out of her, she agreed to let Cocaine come out with them for protection purposes only.

"So, where you wanna go tonight? Limelight will be shakin', bitch!"

"Oh God, I don't know about Limelight, it be so hot in there!"

They were now in the car together, and Cocaine was riding in the backseat cracking up. He didn't care where they were going as long as they got somewhere soon, he was starting to get sick from riding in the backseat for too long.

Lexxy couldn't keep her eyes off Cocaine. She kept watching him from the rearview mirror. She wasn't driving, Denise was, but she kept peaking through the mirror nonetheless. A part of her felt like this was a dream. Cocaine was often in her dreams, running around, being smooth and sexy. She didn't want to admit it to herself, but a part of her missed the little interaction they'd had together, so now that he was back, it was strange, but in a good way.

Cocaine gave her butterflies and wet feelings between her thighs. She enjoyed his company, but he also made her nervous with the way he talked, and he was as fine as could be.

Cocaine noticed Lexxy staring at him, and he flashed her a smile. She quickly tried to look away from the mirror so he wouldn't see her, but it was too late, she'd been spotted.

When they arrived at the club, Cocaine got out first and then went around each side of the door to open them for the ladies. It had been a long time since he'd been to a club, but tonight, he was about to be all about it so he could spend time with the woman of his dreams and her best friend.

The line wasn't long, thank God. They'd arrived at a good time. Cocaine was a little worried about them taking in too much alcohol. He didn't know if Lexxy could turn up, but he could look into Denise's face and tell she was all about a good time. Which was fine as long as everyone was being safe.

Limelight was one of the hottest clubs in the city, so it was packed, but not to the point where they couldn't enjoy themselves. As soon as they got in the door, Denise was at the bar, and then the dance floor, and then back at the door, and Lexxy was following her around like a small puppy just trying to keep up with the action.

Cocaine was trying to give them their space to relax and have a good time. But that was hard to do when they were out on the dance floor, twerking and bouncing around. Men kept coming up to Lexxy, and Cocaine saw her curving them, he couldn't figure out why she was though. Hell, if she didn't wanna fool with him, why would she be pushing these other dudes away. He figured this was his chance to shoot his shot.

"Questions" by Chris Brown came on, and Cocaine walked up to Lexxy, sexy like unbuttoning his shirt as the sweat trickled down his pecks. It was hot as hell in there, and even though he was sexy, he was really just trying to be comfortable.

"Can I have this dance, Miss Lexxy?" he asked as he stuck his hand out to her.

She was a little buzzed, but not drunk, so she smiled, but she hesitated.

"How do I know you can dance, and you don't want

me to just rub my ass on you?" she laughed, causing Cocaine to grab the sides of his ribs to keep from laughing too hard.

"You don't. You just gotta trust me." Cocaine's voice vibrated in her ears, and she didn't want to say it, but she did trust him. She knew somehow that he would take care of her and he would respect her body, and that was what she needed.

The beat dropped several times, and the two of them were glued together, not in a sexual way, but in a sensual and very demanding way. As if their bodies craved one another, but not to be touched, to be loved.

Lexxy's hips swayed back and forth against Cocaine as he had his arms wrapped around her. She smelled like honey, and the smell was making Cocaine weak, but he didn't want Lexxy to know. Denise had told him all about Lucky, and he didn't want her to feel pressured to run into his arms. He wanted her fair and square, not as a second choice. He wasn't the rebound type. He was the first and only type, and he wanted Lexxy to know that, but in her own time, when it was important.

As the song came to a close, Lexxy realized her eyes had been closed the entire time. She had zoned out and was just moving her hips and being happy that everything around her seemed to disappear, and even more so, she lost Denise.

She turned around frantically, looking around the room for her best friend. Cocaine knew what was going on. He'd been watching Denise on and off, keeping up with her since she was a wild child, and ended up dancing with half of the men in the building.

Cocaine leaned down and whispered in her ear:

"She's right behind you, baby. Turn around."

He twisted her hips and turned her back around to face Denise, who was twerking on one guy while using another in front of her for balance.

Lexxy walked up to Denise and gave her a hug. For some reason, she was starting to feel very emotional. The only thing she could think it was, was the gratitude she felt for Denise; for everything, she was doing for her. She'd invited Cocaine, let her stay with her, and she hadn't complained once. She loved Denise and appreciated everything she'd done for her.

Denise was drunk as fuck, sweating the liquor out of her system, and now that she was done dancing, she could hardly stand up straight. Lexxy was trying to hold her up as she walked her through the crowd, but she wasn't strong enough, but Cocaine was. He came right in like a superhero and swept Denise right off her feet and into his arms.

"Come on, baby, let's get y'all home," Cocaine said. He was sad to have to end the night early, but a little time with Lexxy was like a lifetime in heaven, it was perfect.

Lexxy ran to the car and opened the door up for Cocaine so he could slide Denise into the car. He placed her inside and slowly shut the door, being careful not to hit her head because she was slipping down quickly.

Lexxy sat in the back with Denise, stroking her hair and fanning her, so she didn't throw up as Cocaine drove them home. Lexxy was giving him directions as they went through the streets, and they even made some small talk here and there, trying to get to know one another.

When they arrived at Denise's house, Cocaine got out of the car, grabbed Denise and carried her up the stairs to her apartment as Lexxy opened the door.

"Here, you can just sit her right here. She'll want to be close to the kitchen and the bathroom for when she finally is able to move," Lexxy said as she covered her mouth to stifle a laugh from coming out.

Cocaine nodded and gently put her on the couch. Lexxy wondered if this was what it would be like to come home drunk with Cocaine. If he would be as gentle with her as he was being with Denise. She'd never had anything like that before. Lucky always made fun of her if she came home too drunk, so this was all brand new to her.

Lexxy covered her up and tiptoed outside with Cocaine.

"I can give you a ride back to your car if you want?" Lexxy asked.

"Nah, I'ma catch a Lyft, stay here with your friend."

Lexxy wanted to be in there with Denise, but she also wanted to be out here, to be with Cocaine.

"Well, why don't we just sit in the car and talk for a little while? Is that ok?"

"It's more than cool with me, ma."

Cocaine couldn't believe he was voluntarily getting some of her time. He loved it, and he was going to milk it for all it was worth.

While they were in the car, they talked about everything, laughed about everything, and truly enjoyed each other's company, so much so that the sun rising over the horizon didn't make either one of them stop talking, nor did it make them want to be apart.

Now that Lexxy had spent the last few hours with him, she learned how smart and funny he was. How charming he could be outside of how he already was, and she learned about his parents, and though she had parents, she would've given anything for a mother who was active in her life instead of one that was always gone.

It was seven a.m, and Denise had finally come to. She wobbled around the house looking for Lexxy, and when she didn't find her, she opened the door to see if her car was still outside, both vehicles were. Not only did she find the cars, but Lexxy and Cocaine were inside of one, talking and laughing.

She hobbled down the stairs, one by one and went up to the window, knocking loudly on it.

Lexxy was startled as she turned around to see who it was.

"Denise! What are you doin'? You scared the shit out of me!"

"Mhmm…you ain't livin' right, that's why. Girl, y'all sittin' out here like some teenagers, why don't y'all come inside?"

Though it shouldn't have been a big deal, it was a major one to Lexxy. Was Cocaine going to come inside? What if he didn't want to? This was going to let Lexxy know a lot about him. If he couldn't come in and chill with them, he probably wasn't that social, and she needed a social, happy man in her life. Not someone who was shy and closed off. She liked to talk, and so far, it seemed like Cocaine did too.

CHAPTER 12

"I mean, if it's cool with y'all, I don't mind."

And there it was. Lexxy was surprised, but at the same time, she really wasn't. She was happy that he was going to come in, but now she was starting to try to remember if the house was clean. Had she remembered to pick it up before they left the house to go to her graduation? She didn't want anybody coming in when it was a mess, when it was disgusting. Though Denise and Lexxy were females, they worked a lot and were always gone, so sometimes, they forgot to clean the house.

Cocaine could see the fear on Lexxy's face, and he wanted to reassure her.

"It's cool. I'm not inspecting your spot. I don't care what you got goin' on. I'm not tryna be all in your business. If y'all don't want me to come in…"

"We do, we do, right, Denise?" Lexxy said trying to get Denise on her side, but she already was whether she realized it or not. She saw something good in Cocaine, something different, something that she knew her best friend needed. Lexxy had been with Lucky way too long, and she wanted her to be with someone new. Someone worthy of being with, and she could see that in Cocaine.

Hell, he was already stepping up to the plate by being their security last night, and he didn't have to do that.

"Of course we do. Why don't you come in, and I can make us all breakfast."

"Or I can," Lexxy announced. For some reason, she was feeling the strangest urge to prove herself to Cocaine. Since they'd stayed up all night talking, she had new-found feelings for him. He was really funny and very caring, and he seemed to have a good head on his shoulders, minus the fact that he was selling drugs and had come up here from Texas. Lexxy had always heard people from Texas were not nice, and they weren't to be trusted, but so far, everyone she'd met seemed to be cool, and she could only count Cocaine in the people she knew from Texas.

"Ok, girl, you got it. It's all you!"

Denise wasn't going to argue. She didn't feel like making breakfast for anyone but herself, so the simple fact that she volunteered to cook for everyone just made it that much better.

Cocaine stepped into the house, and he couldn't tell the night before, but the apartment was very nice and well decorated. It smelled like women lived there with the scented candles and all the different smells of incense burning.

"Here, have a seat on the couch," Denise said as she patted the seat next to her, fluffing the cushion up for him.

"Cool."

Cocaine sat down next to Denise as he watched

Lexxy in the kitchen starting to pull out the dishes from underneath the cabinet and the food out of the fridge.

"Sausage, eggs, and pancakes ok?"

"Whatever you make is ok," Cocaine said with a wink. Meanwhile, Denise was on the other side of him doing some strange dance letting her know that she was all for them being together. She was making weird faces that only Lexxy would understand, but when Cocaine turned back around, she was looking normal again.

"So, what do y'all have planned for the day, Miss Lexxy?"

She blushed when he called her that, and she shrugged her shoulders.

"I didn't have anything planned I guess. I was just going to relax the day away. I have a few days 'til I start working at Baptist, so I was just going to relax until it was time."

"Shit, I was just goin' lay around till work tonight honestly," Denise said as she threw her feet up on the coffee table to rest them and add emphasis to her laying around.

"What do you have planned, Cocaine?"

"Shit, I'm tryna be up under you all day for real. Y'all wanna go shoppin'?"

As soon as Cocaine said it, he was just as surprised as anyone else. He'd never taken a woman shopping, but for Lexxy, he would give her the world. Even if she already had it.

Denise hearing the word shopping was like hearing she'd won the lottery. It had been a long time since she had a man show her any attention, even in a friendly way. So she wasn't goin' turn this down, not for nothin' in the world, wasn't no way.

"Uuhm, I'm definitely in, as long as Lexx is in."

"I mean, I don't know what I would buy seeing as how most of my clothes will be scrubs from now on," she admitted. Plus, she didn't want to spend his money. She didn't know what he was working with financially, and it wasn't her business.

"True, but you still might see somethin' you like, and you can have whatever you want," he said as he looked in her direction; almost making her burn the sausage.

Denise was behind him with her tongue stuck out, lightly bouncing around so he wouldn't feel it. She was too hype, and she just hoped Lexxy didn't let this one go.

"Breakfast is almost ready. Cocaine, if you wanna change your clothes, I got some of my cousin's stuff upstairs. He stays here from time to time when he's in the city."

Cocaine didn't feel comfortable puttin' on another man's clothes. It wasn't that big of a deal; he could just buy himself some more when they got to the mall and change into them.

Denise directed him upstairs and told him where he could find everything. As soon as he disappeared upstairs, she flew around the corner and started laughing.

"Bbbiiitttcchhh! I think you got a keeper! You gave him some, didn't you? Ooh you nasty, in the car?"

"Denise, shut up! I didn't give anybody anything, and you know it. He's just…nice I guess."

"Just nice? Bitch, are you blind? He is the one. Come on now, don't be bein' stupid. I tried to warn you about

Lucky, and I'm sorry I keep bringin' it up. But come on now, God closed a door and opened a window for you. Crawl your chocolate ass into that window and get your man!"

Denise was spitting straight facts at Lexxy, and it was up to her to take them…or not.

Breakfast was ready, and Cocaine had come down just in time. His body was glistening as he threw his shirt over his arms just before he sat down at the table. Both Denise and Lexxy's mouths were agape.

They sat down at the table, and Cocaine looked at the food, pleased with how it looked and smelled, he just hoped it tasted good too.

Though Lexxy and Denise had full plates, they sat there, slowly eating, mainly watching Cocaine enjoy the food.

"Y'all ok?" he asked, looking up from his food with a mouth stuffed full of eggs.

"Yeah, we're good," Lexxy said as she looked over at Denise who was still watching him eat.

"So, I'm gonna go ahead and start getting ready. Denise, you wanna help me?"

"No!"

Lexxy looked over at Denise who was intently staring at Cocaine. So Lexxy asked again.

"Don't you wanna help me?" Denise looked in Lexxy's direction and rolled her eyes.

"I guess so. I didn't want to, but I guess I will."

"If you wanna watch TV, you can, or just do whatever. We'll be back in a minute. Just make yourself comfortable."

Denise and Lexxy stood up from the table. As Lexxy passed by his seat, he grabbed her wrist, making her stop dead in her tracks.

"Thank you for breakfast, beautiful."

Lexxy nervously smiled and walked off, running upstairs like a teenage girl. It felt good to have someone to flirt with; it was all harmless, right?

Lexxy showered, put her clothes on, did her makeup and hair in less than an hour. Which was rare for her, but she didn't want to be away from Cocaine. He was contagious, and his conversation was intoxicating. She would take up all of his time if she could.

When she finally made it downstairs, Denise was already down there looking for her shoes and purse, and Cocaine was trying to help her find them.

"Here's your purse!" Cocaine was proud of himself for finding it since he didn't even remember her having one on the night before. But when he laid eyes on Lexxy, the wheels in his mind started turning, she was beautiful and shining brighter than a diamond.

"Miss Lexxy, you goin' make me regret leaving my gun in my car. You goin' have me fightin' niggas off you all day," he said as he walked closer to her, trying to get a better look.

Her outfit was simple. She wore an all-white body suit with blue jean shorts and her all-white Jordan's, but she just looked good in them. Cocaine could appreciate a simply beautiful woman.

Lexxy blushed and hit him across the chest. He was joking, but not really. He was the type to shoot first and ask questions later.

Denise found her shoes, and Lexxy and Cocaine were both ready to go. She couldn't say officially, but this shit seemed almost like a date. She didn't want to jump the gun though and embarrass herself in case it wasn't.

When they got to Opry Mills Lexxy didn't know where she wanted to go. What stores should she shop in? She had a pretty good idea of where she could go, but she also wasn't sure of her budget. She didn't want to seem high maintenance, although she was. She could afford to be, but she didn't know what Cocaine had in his pockets.

"So, where y'all wanna go?" Cocaine asked them both but looked at Lexxy.

"Uhm…well, I love Lush. Why don't we go in there first? We can get some stuff for our skin and some new soaps and stuff."

"Ooh yes, girl. We gotta get that golden bath bubble bar thing. Shit had me looking like a natural highlighter for a week," Denise said, but she wasn't lying. The golden bubble bar was everytttthhhhing.

Cocaine walked behind them, watching to make sure they were safe, even if they didn't know it. Cocaine always felt like someone was watching him, or even other people, they just didn't know. So he took it as his personal job to watch out for them, especially after Lexxy told him she was rich. He figured a rich girl probably always had a target on her back, and he wanted to make sure he could kill a crisis before one even arose. He didn't care about her having money, or going to a good school. He had his own money, so that shit didn't matter. What he cared about was how she handled herself and how she acted, and so far, from what he could see, she was handling things just fine.

When they made it to Lush, Cocaine felt like eyes were on them, so he looked around, trying to see if he could see anyone, but he didn't. Well he didn't see anyone that seemed suspicious. But someone was watching them, so he stuck close to Denise and Lexxy in case some shit went down.

After they'd got their stuff rang up, and Cocaine paid for it in cash, they left the store and went out into the halls of the mall. Lexxy was laughing and locked arms with Denise on one side, and she was extremely close to Cocaine on the other when she saw a familiar face, several at that.

Right across from them was Lucky, Carley, and their little boy. They looked like such a happy family, and Lexxy couldn't stand it, but she also didn't want to be seen by Lucky either. She hoped he didn't see her because she didn't want him to see the look of anger, rage, and sadness spread across her cheeks. She quickly broke arms with Denise and turned around, walking off.

"Lexxy! Lex, wait!" Denise called out to her, only making it worse. Lucky turned around in the direction he heard Denise's voice, and he came right into eye contact with Cocaine. Cocaine smiled a devilish smile and threw his hand up before going after Lexxy.

He didn't know why Lexxy walked away like that, but not that he did, he was happy to have seen Lucky. He was going to be feeling sick to his stomach. He didn't want Lexxy around Cocaine, but what choice did he have now? She was a free agent and allowed to do what her heart desired. Lucky was going to have to deal with that, after all, he was living his life, however, he saw fit.

Cocaine caught up with Lexxy and Denise, and Lexxy was almost in tears.

"I mean, I knew I'd probably eventually see him, but I didn't know it would be all of them together. I don't want to see them, ever again. Did you see how happy he looked? He was smiling."

Cocaine knew this wasn't the time to spout no charming shit at her. She needed to hear the truth, and he knew all about what happened because once again, Denise couldn't keep her mouth shut.

"On some real shit, if the nigga was stuntin' you, or worried about you he would've never let you go. The moment he fucked up, he would've been sick to death about it. He would've been begging to come back home and make the shit work, and he ain't do that, bae. You gotta let his lame ass go, not even for our sake, but for your sake. You goin' miserable forever? You can't let somebody who was never really meant to have you keep you."

The tears flew freely from Lexxy's eyes, and she was trying to calm down because she was embarrassed to be breaking down like this in front of Cocaine. The more she cried, he just held her in his arms, kissing her forehead.

"Come on, bae, you gotta get out of eye view. Don't give that nigga the satisfaction of seeing you cry. Understand?"

Lexxy nodded her head and allowed Cocaine to help her move from the spot she was in. She felt so weak and so unhappy. She never wanted to see Lucky again, especially not lookin' all happy with his family and shit. Lexxy couldn't help but wonder how much worse this could have been had Cocaine not been there. She probably would've flipped out and beat Lucky's ass.

Yes, Lexxy knew that Lucky didn't cheat on her, but the simple fact that he was sneaking around, that was what really bothered her. She felt like they had lost all the trust they had at one point. Which made a lot of sense because of how strangely he was acting, but she wondered why he was so willing to settle down and be with this woman. He was with Lexxy for five years, and he could never seem to make it work. Was it her? Even if it wasn't, she always felt like it was.

No matter how hard Lexxy tried, she was never enough. She could never get Lucky to behave the way he should have. Denise told her to chalk it up to him just being an idiot. She wanted to believe that, but how could she?

Lexxy wanted to leave the mall, but Denise wasn't having that. They hadn't been there long, and they'd only been to one store.

"Uhn-uhn, bitch. Don't let him ruin your day. We ain't been shoppin' in so long because we ain't had time. Now we got some, and you wanna leave. Get yo' shit together!"

Denise tried to encourage her bestie because she didn't know the next time they were going to get offered an opportunity like this to shop on the next muthafucka's dime. They both had money in the bank, but who really wants to spend their own money? Nobody.

Lexxy turned to look at Cocaine, and he grabbed her hand.

"If you want to, we can. We can go home, or we can keep shoppin'. Whatever you want."

Cocaine saying the word home both made them pause. Lexxy loved the way it sounded coming out of his mouth. Cocaine wished his home was the same place she was going to be. He was falling for Lexxy, especially after last night. Now that she had to deal with this fuck boy Lucky, he just wanted to do anything to make her happy. He'd kill him if she would ok it.

"I-I guess we can keep shopping," Lexxy finally said. She stood up from the bench she was on, pulled her shorts down that were now riding up in her ass, and she took off walking with Denise and Cocaine.

She never let Cocaine's hand go, and he never said anything about it.

"Aye, boss, guess who I just saw?"

"Who?"

"Lexxy….but she wasn't with that fool Lucky."

"Who was she with then?"

"That dude I told you about from the hospital, and they were holding hands. Shit, I guess it must be gettin' serious."

Wild Bill was on the phone with Dutch giving him the details on what Lexxy was doing. Because Lexxy's family came from money, her father always worried about new people coming into her life. He always thought they all wanted something from her when that wasn't necessarily the case. For the most part, she hardly told people she was rich. She usually just kept it to herself and only told the people around her who she felt could handle it. She was smart enough to know that most people couldn't take something like that. She didn't even like to tempt people with shit like that. Although she was about that life and could get with a muthafucka, she didn't want to have to. Hell, she was almost thirty after all.

"Mhmm…and what do we know about him?"

"Nothin' at all. Shit, I know his name, but I met 'em, and the

nigga seemed like he might be alright. I don't know if it's worth causin' no problems over."

"Just watch them and get me some information on this nigga. I need to know who's around my daughter at all times. You said this nigga seems like a street cat, right? Follow the blueprint. I wanna know who his people are, who he fucks with, what he wants. Matter fact, you keep followin' them and make sure baby girl is ok, I'ma call her ass right now."

Dutch hung up in Wild Bill's face, and he just shook his head. He was protective over Lexxy too, but damn, he let her live a little, and the only reason he called to tell Dutch was because everyone was ready for her to move on from Lucky. They all worried she wouldn't be able to be with anyone else, or she would be with someone else that would do the same thing or use her for her money.

Wild Bill just hoped for Lexxy's sake that Cocaine was in it to win it. That he wasn't on no stupid shit because her father was a man of means, and he had some real killas on his side that would do whatever it took if somebody crossed his baby. Wild Bill was one of them.

Lexxy, Denise, and Cocaine were back walking through the mall, having the time of their lives. Cocaine was still holding Lexxy's hand every chance he got. He was holding all of her things while she shopped till she dropped. She was having more fun than she'd had even the night before. Denise was racking up, and she had all types of stuff; watches, shoes, clothes, everything you could imagine.

After walking around all day, Lexxy was hungry. She was ready to sit her skinny ass down and eat something before she passed out, so she let go of Cocaine's hand and ran straight to the Panda Express so she could fill that little belly of hers. Cocaine and Denise followed behind her, ordering their food after she did.

When Lexxy got her food and sat down, she made sure there was enough room for all of her bags, and for Cocaine and Denise, and then she dug in. She had already waited too long to eat, and she was about to start getting hangry any second now. Not hungry, but hangry. Angry and hungry at the same damn time, and that could be a dangerous thing.

Cocaine watched Lexxy eat her food, and he thought she was so cute. She had a small mouth so that meant she couldn't chew that big, and she couldn't put that much food in her mouth at one time. She kept a napkin in her lap for the most part, which was hilarious to him because she was such a neat eater. She didn't even need the napkin, for real.

As she sat there eating her food, watching Cocaine watch her, she felt her phone vibrating in her pocket. She pulled it out and rolled her eyes. It was her father calling. She hadn't spoken with him since she ended up at Denise's, and she didn't think this was a good time to be talking to him. If she didn't answer now, he would just keep on calling, and that was the last thing she wanted. She didn't want him to keep calling and bothering her, so she went ahead and answered the phone--so he could say what he needed to, and so she could go on about her day.

"Hello, Daddy," Lexxy answered, rolling her eyes.

"Hey, baby girl, what ya' doin'?" he asked, his voice low and gruff.

"Uhm, nothing. At the mall, shopping."

"Shopping you said? Maybe I should come. I haven't gotten to spend money on my little girl in quite some time."

Lexxy felt the panic in her begin to rise. She knew how he could be about the guys she dated. If she could even call what her and Cocaine were doing dating. Especially since she had a little episode about Lucky before.

"Oh, you know, Daddy, we're just about to leave. Don't worry about it. Maybe you and I can go another day."

"Who is we? Who you out there with, baby?"

Damn, her daddy was pressing her, and she honestly didn't want to tell him anything because she knew how he could be. But what she didn't know was Wild Bill had already seen her and was already watching her whether she wanted him to be or not.

"Denise, Daddy. Me and Denise."

"Oh, tell my other daughter I said hello. You girls be good, won't you?"

"Always, Daddy. I'm always good."

Dutch held the phone in his hand, close to his face, trying to decide if he should mention the fact that he knew she was there with a man, and he decided he should.

"So, baby, tell me about this new nigga that you've been hanging out with, Cocaine? Who names their child that?"

Lexxy almost spit her food out when she heard her father mention him by name. She tried laughing it off, and she put her finger up in the air, signaling she'd be back in a minute. When she walked away from the table, she looked at the phone, and anger filled her.

"Daddy, is that why you called? To pester me about someone?"

"Hell yeah, I wanna know what he wants with you, baby. Why is he hanging around you? What does he want?"

"Because someone can't want to just be around me, I guess. Excuse me."

"They can, but this nigga fell out of the sky it seems like. Where did he come from?"

Lexxy didn't feel like she needed to explain herself. Especially when she didn't even know what was going on with her and Cocaine. She liked him, a lot, but she was damaged. Even though Lexxy didn't know it, he was too. Cocaine had some inner demons that he was dealing with himself. They were destined to come out at some point, but until her and Cocaine got serious, if they ever decided to, she didn't feel like she owed her father an explanation or any details on their relationship, at least not for now.

"Daddy, I'm not about to explain myself to you. I'm an adult, and I don't owe you shit. I know you think I need to be protected, but I promise you, I'm doing just fine on my own. Please let me live and let me grow up. I'm almost thirty years old, Dutch!"

She was really mad now. She only called her father by his real name when she got really mad, but he was pushing her. He was taking her to a place she hated to go. Lexxy idn't want to seem like a bitch, but damn. At what point did he realize she wasn't a child and that she could fight her own battles, no matter how they came?

"Just mind your business, Daddy, because for now, there isn't even any business to tell!"

She hit the end button and hung up the phone. Lexxy was glad her back was facing the other way so no one could see her, or at least she thought. When she turned around, she came face to face with Cocaine. He startled her, making her jump, and her phone fell out of her hand as she yelped.

"Damn it, Cocaine! What are you doing?" she asked nervously.

"You were throwing your arms all up in the air, so I assumed you were upset. I came over to check on you, but I was trnna give you some space at the same time."

Lexxy couldn't believe this. A man she'd known only a month, was being nicer to her and more considerate than the nigga she was with for five years. Maybe it was time for her to move on, and maybe it could be with Cocaine.

"Thank you for checking on me. I'm ok, I promise."

"Ok, good. You wanna finish shoppin', or you done for the day?"

Lexxy thought about it, and she didn't want Cocaine to go home. She'd spent the whole day with him, again, but it wasn't enough time. She didn't want him to go home, but she didn't want to seem thirsty or needy. She took too long to respond, so Cocaine knew she must have been thinking.

"Well, I don't think I could buy anything else. Maybe we could go bowling or something like that."

Cocaine knew what was going on. She didn't want him to leave, and he didn't want to either. He also needed to go home and get some of his own clothes if he was going to be hanging out with her. He still hadn't changed out of Denise's cousin's clothes yet.

"I mean, you could come back to the house if you want, or we could go out, just me and you…"

"Ooh, is my baby asking me on a date?"

She couldn't deny that she was, nor that she didn't like hearing the word baby because she did. She liked him treating her like she was his. Whether she knew it or not, she was. Her cheeks burned with heat as he put her on front street, but it was true, she was asking him out, so she shook her head up and down because she couldn't speak any words. At least not any English in that moment.

In that moment, he found her to be more beautiful than before. Maybe he was just tired, but she looked different to him, and he wasn't goin' let this moment pass him up.

He pulled her into him and planted his lips firmly but passionately on hers. She received him like she'd been hungry for his lips instead of the food. He wrapped his arms around her waist, and then down to her ass, squeezing her cheeks. She let out a slight moan, and his dick began peeking through his pants. His erection was making her mind go crazy with wild thoughts. She hadn't had sex in so long, and she was so horny. She didn't want to come off as a thot, so she separated herself from him, wiped her lips, and pulled her shorts back down.

When they stepped away from each other, Denise

popped her head in the middle, breaking their concentration from one another.

“Now, if you two nasties are done…” She raised her hand, motioning for them to walk toward the right back to the car.

Lexxy burst out laughing, and Cocaine smacked her ass and then grabbed her hand. Lexxy wasn’t used to this public display of affection. Lucky had always said he didn’t like it, but the shit had her hot and heavy and turned her on.

The kiss Lexxy and Cocaine shared was so passionate. There was no way that the answer to a date was a no. It was a hell yes, but he had to go home and get his shit together first. He couldn't be going out with her looking like a scrub, so they went back to Denise's house and made plans for later on that evening.

"Thank you for today, Cocaine! I had a good time!" Denise yelled over her shoulder as she walked up the stairs to her apartment.

Lexxy got out of the car and was going up the stairs when Cocaine grabbed her by her belt loop and pulled her back towards him.

"So, you was gon' just go in the house without saying bye?"

She looked down at her shoes. It had been a long time since Lexxy flirted with anyone other than Lucky. Even though she should've been used to it by now with Cocaine, she just wasn't. She liked him a lot, but he made her nervous. Every moment they were together, it was like an emotional menopause. That was one reason why she liked him. She figured things would never get old, and he was corny, but in the best way he could be. He said smooth shit that turned her on, and certain things there was just no way of ignoring. Just like when he gave her the watch. She had been thinking of him ever since it was given to her. She had been thinking a lot about time since the watch was given to her, but that was one of the best gifts anyone had ever given her.

"No, I wasn't. I was just—"

Cocaine grabbed her again, licking her bottom lip, and then sucked it into his. He'd been waiting an hour to do it again, and an hour was way too long.

"You were just what? Runnin' from me?" he said as he pulled his lips away from hers and held her.

"I don't know, Cocaine. I don't know what I'm doing." Lexxy shrugged her shoulders. She wasn't sure what she was doing, what she was feeling, nor what she should be doing with Cocaine.

"I know you don't. That's why you need to let me lead, and you follow, baby. I got you. Now, you mentioned going on a date? You want me to take you out tonight? We can grab some dinner or somethin'?"

Lexxy thought about where she wanted to eat. The truth was, the only place she wanted to eat was only open from midnight to three a.m today. She had a hankering for breakfast, and she was determined to get it.

"How about we grab a late/ early breakfast if you're up?"

Cocaine looked confused.

"What do you mean, if I'm up?"

"If you're up. I mean, if you are, then we can go to Monell's. Have you been?"

Cocaine hadn't been anywhere really. He'd been so thirsty for revenge; he wasn't worried about the rest. But now, since Lexxy was giving him some time, he would do whatever it took to be with her, however he needed to.

"Nah, I haven't been yet. What time you tryna go?"

"They don't open 'tll midnight," Lexxy said as she put her hand up to her mouth. She had never been on an actual date that late. She didn't want to give Cocaine the wrong impression or make it seem like she was easy because she was going out that late.

"Ok, cool. Give me your phone, baby, so I can text you all day 'til we go out," Cocaine said smiling. He was dead ass serious. From the moment Lexxy gave him her phone number, he was texting her. He called a Lyft to pick him up, and Lexxy waited outside with him for it to come, but as it did, they sent each other little text messages, even though they were right beside one another.

Lexxy couldn't wait to go on a date with Cocaine. She knew he knew how to have a good time, and he was a gentleman. She looked forward to spending time with him and getting to know him. Though he was taking a Lyft back to his car, Lexxy wanted to give him a ride, but he said no. That it wasn't necessary. He wanted her to rest up for their date that night because he planned on spending the entire night with her, either at his place or hers.

Cocaine was never going to let Lexxy go, and she needed to understand that. He just hoped after he told her his secret that she'd be able to deal with it, and she wouldn't run away. He had a good feeling about her. He just knew somehow that she would be down to ride, but his suspicions would either be confirmed or denied after midnight.

After a full day of sleeping, Lexxy got up, showered, and put on a sundress. It was eleven o'clock, and it was still hot as the devil's ball sack outside. Her army green sundress meshed well with her dark skin, and you know she was glowing. She had on brown gladiator sandals that strapped all the way up her legs to her knees. Her dress was long in the back and cut short in the front. Her hair was down and wavy, surrounding her shoulders, at least that's what she decided on once she'd flipped and brushed and gelled it down a hundred times.

She hated to admit it, but damn was she nervous. She was so afraid of going on this date and making a fool of herself. But at the same time, she felt like it was time. She didn't want to be alone forever, and she didn't eventually want to be old and alone. The only way that was going to happen was if she opened her heart up to someone, and why shouldn't it be Cocaine? He was fine, had money, smart, could make her laugh, and he was always there. She just knew he wouldn't emotionally check out on her the way Lucky had at the end of their relationship.

Lexxy wanted to tell Denise she was about to leave, but she was knocked out. She didn't want to disturb her, so she waited until Cocaine texted and said he was outside, and then she tiptoed out the door. They'd been texting all day. She was waking up out of her sleep to text him back, and when he didn't text her back right away, she assumed he was asleep. But she didn't want to ask or be in his business because she didn't feel she had the right to just yet. She would wait until the time was right if the time ever came.

When she got outside, Cocaine was leaned against the car with a long linen shirt on, with the matching linen pants on and a black pair of Jordan's, with the hanging gold chain. That boy could really dress. Lexxy's eyes lit up when she saw him. She wanted to run out to him and jump into his arms, but she was trying to follow his lead like he said before. She didn't want to do too much, so she slowly walked down the steps and decided to just give him a small hug. She turned to the side and wrapped one arm around him with her booty poked out the other way.

He smirked and turned her around and put his arms around her waist. She returned the gesture by placing her head on his chest and hugging him back tightly.

"I don't know why you just tried to play me with that church hug, bae. Get yo' fine ass in this car so I can take you to get some food. I'm glad we comin' out late. I don't want nobody to see you lookin' all good. I been done had to knock somebody out on our date."

"Cocaine, shut up! Don't nobody want me."

"Shit, I do, and if I do, I know other niggas do. Unless they got bad taste or they gay."

Lexxy laughed as Cocaine opened the door for her and she slid in.

When they pulled up to Monell's, there were only three cars outside. Very few people knew about this treasure in Nashville. So at night time, it was often slept on. It was Lexxy's favorite place, so she ate there more than she ate at home sometimes.

Cocaine and Lexxy went inside and the hostess, Gloria, directed them to a table. Monell's was a southern style buffet where they served biscuits and gravy, fried chicken no matter the occasion, corn pudding, bacon, sausage, country ham, fried apples, breakfast potatoes, and eggs. Normally you would sit with people you didn't know and pass the food around the table, but there was no one else in there with them, which was good for what Cocaine wanted to tell Lexxy.

After sitting down at the table, and Cocaine saw all the food they were about to eat, he looked at his pants and shook his head.

"Damn baby, I don't know if I wore the right shit to be tryna consume all this food. You goin' have me out here lookin' all fat and shit."

"Don't worry about your weight, Cocaine. I love you either way."

She was stuffing food in her mouth as she said it, and Cocaine smiled at her. She had completely missed the fact that she said that.

"What?" she asked with her face twisted up.

"Nothin', baby, so look, I wanna tell you somethin'," Cocaine said, shaking off what Lexxy secretly announced. He wanted to go ahead and get it off his chest before shit went south.

"Ok, what's up?" she asked, her face completely in the food.

"So, you know I came up here from Houston, right?"

"Uhm-hum, what about it?"

"The reason I came up here is because I'm lookin' for the man who killed my father."

Lexxy put her fork down and looked into his eyes. It wasn't that she didn't know Cocaine's father had passed away or even that he had been murdered, because she did, but him looking for the man? That was like a huge bomb that had been dropped on her.

"And do you know who he is?"

"Yeah, and I know where he is…"

"And what do you plan on doing?" Lexxy asked in a hushed tone, in case one of the three other people in the restaurant could hear her.

"I'ma wack that nigga and put 'em in the dirt. Or I might kill him and have the body put somewhere to rot. He don't deserve to go back to the earth, baby. He killed my daddy in cold blood on some sneak shit."

Lexxy nodded her head and kept eating. She didn't say anything else, and that worried Cocaine. But he didn't know what to say. He wanted this date to be fun for her, and so they could continue to enjoy each other, but he also wanted to be honest. He didn't want to keep any secrets from her, even if she didn't like what she heard.

"Sexy Lexxy, what you thinkin' 'bout?" he asked her as he reached for her hand. She put her fork down and placed her hand on top of his, looking into his eyes.

"I don't know what it's like to lose a parent, so I can't

say I wouldn't do the same thing in your position. I'm not judging you, so I don't want you to think that. I want you to be careful, Cocaine. Vengeance is all fun and games 'til somebody gets hurt. So, just be careful. I'd hate for something to happen to you before we get to go on another date." Lexxy laughed.

Cocaine knew Lexxy was cool. He knew something was different about her and that she was down. He then proceeded to ask another question.

"So, if I go to jail for murder, not that I'll get caught, but if I do, you gon' write me and come see a nigga?"

"I mean, if I don't, who else will?" she asked seriously. She wanted to know if there were other women in the background of what they could having going on. Lexxy wouldn't play second. She was an ONLY type of chick; a priority, not an option.

"It ain't nobody in my life but you, woman. Shit, you ain't even goin' all the way, but I'm confident. I know you just been hurt, and you ain't all the way over that shit. I'ma give you some time 'til you're ready."

"Are you? I thought you would just take me now that I'm a free agent."

Cocaine threw his hands up. He couldn't win with this girl.

"You don't know what you want, do you? I ain't gon' let you bother me, Sexy Lexxy. In my mind, you're already mine. As soon as you accept that, we'll be good."

Cocaine knew he saw something special in her that day at the diner. He knew she was different from anyone he'd ever met, and he had to keep her in his life. Once all this shit was over with, with the man who killed his father, he was going to be ready to settle down on some family shit, so he hoped Lexxy was ready. He would love to penetrate her gene pool because he knew the babies would be smart, beautiful, and royalty.

"I do know what I want; I just don't show it the way you do."

Even though Lexxy said that, she was about to make a very bold move to show him how much she liked him. How she actually wanted to spend time with him, more time than now.

"And to show you I do know what I want and that I do actually like you, why don't you come back to my house? We can watch some movies or play cards, or whatever you want."

"Whatever I want?" Cocaine asked with raised eyebrows.

"Within certain limits, of course," Lexxy said, lowering her head to give him the illusion that she was serious.

"Yeah, that's what you better say, Lexxy."

They finished up their meal, and Lexxy shared with Cocaine her dreams to open her own private practice and to be amongst the other three female black surgeons before they were thirty. That was her goal, and she was going to make it. She just had to find more time to go back to school while working at the hospital now. Though she was certified to be an OGBYN and a medical practitioner, she didn't have the proper degree nor was she comfortable enough yet to be a surgeon. That didn't matter though because she was smart, and anything she put her mind to, she could have and would do.

Cocaine seemed to almost speed home when they left the restaurant. He couldn't wait to get into her room to see what it looked like. He wanted to know what she liked, what she disliked, how she slept when she was at home instead of in a hospital, and how comfortable she would be sleeping close to him, if they made it to the sleeping part. Cocaine wanted to know everything about her, no matter what it was.

Cocaine parked the car, and they walked into the house together. Denise was still dead to the world, which was probably better for Lexxy. She would have been really embarrassed if Denise would have seen her coming in the house with Cocaine. She would've made it into something it wasn't.

Lexxy and Cocaine both sat their keys on the table near the door and went upstairs to Lexxy's room. She cut the light on, and the room looked exactly like Cocaine thought it would. It had bright colors all over the walls, the sheets were black and white, matching pillowcases, matching rugs and all.

"If you need to go to the bathroom, you can just go through that door."

"I'm good, baby. Your room is cute, though. Look at you, like a lil' teenager. You got a diary up here somewhere filled with my name in it?"

She couldn't believe he was asking her that. What kind of woman would just openly admit having a diary? Even more so, why would she show it to him?

"If I did, you wouldn't know it. That isn't your business. Now come sit down. I'll cut a movie on."

Cocaine came and sat down on the bed and took his shoes off, propped himself up on her pillows, and got comfortable.

"Think you're at home, don't ya'?"

"Shit, I am. What we finna watch, bae?"

Lexxy loved his confidence. It did something to her insides, and she was really starting to like Cocaine.

She pulled out her favorite movie, 'Night at the Museum' with Ben Stiller and put it in.

"You ever seen this?"

"Hell nah, but Ben Stiller is a funny cat, so I ain't trippin'. Plus, whatever you wanna do is cool by me, baby."

Lexxy took off her shoes and slid into her bed next to Cocaine, but still at the opposite side of the bed. Cocaine noticed how far away she was and he reached out and pulled her close to him. Lexxy hadn't been this close to a man since Lucky. No matter how close she was to Lucky, physically, mentally, emotionally, she couldn't help but feel like this was different. Cocaine made her feel things she'd never felt before, and that almost scared her. He gave her butterflies and almost made her feel nauseous with excitement, something she wasn't used to feeling, but she loved it.

Though the movie was on, neither one of them were able to really focus on the screen. They kept looking at each other, and their minds were both turning like little hamster wheels thinking of one another. Lexxy's mind was in the gutter. She didn't want it to be, but she couldn't help it. While she was lying on Cocaine's chest, she could see his dick starting to rise. From the looks of it, it was thick, and she wanted to see the rest, but she didn't want to be aggressive with Cocaine. She still hardly knew him, and she didn't want to come across as a hoe. She didn't need that, but Cocaine peeped what she was doing. She kept moving so she could see it, and she even put her leg over his waist. What did she think that was going to do to him?

He didn't want to test Lexxy to see how far she'd let shit go, but he did wanna kiss her, so he did. He turned over and started kissing her. It was slow and steady at first, and Lexxy still had her leg around him, but now her pussy was lined up with his dick, and they could feel each other's warmth. As they kissed, the wetness from their mouths drenched each other's lips, creating a passionate tension between the two.

Cocaine was grabbing at Lexxy's ass, and she was grabbing on his shirt. They were pulling each other into the other, closing in the space between them. The more they kissed, the hotter it became, but it was a good heat.

Though Lexxy said she wasn't going to be all aggressive, her clit was telling her to do otherwise. It was tingling, and her pussy was wet without it even being touched yet. She used her strength and climbed on top of Cocaine, and his dick jumped as she sat on it.

Cocaine felt like a little kid about to dry hump his girlfriend. He was trying to keep it cool. He didn't wanna look like a lame who couldn't control his dick. As good as she felt on top of him, he needed to be in control, so he flipped her over on her back and laid beside her.

Lexxy had never been kissed this way. Cocaine's mouth enveloped both of her lips, and his breath smelled like mint, which made it that much easier to want to kiss him.

Lexxy's breasts were falling out of her dress from all of the moving around she'd done. Cocaine wanted to respect her body, but he wanted to suck on her nipples. Earlier that day, when they were at the mall, her nipples had gotten hard, and they were big like quarters. He wanted to taste them and squeeze them until she couldn't take it anymore. While her eyes were closed, and he was kissing her, Cocaine flicked her nipples between his fingertips, and her eyes popped open. She watched him as much as she could until it was too much to bear. She wiggled all over the bed the harder her nipples got. Her pussy was pulsating, beating like a heartbeat.

He slipped her giant, chocolate gum ball nipples in his mouth, and Lexxy almost jumped out of bed. One at a time, he sucked and licked.

"Mmm…suck harder," she moaned, and he did as she commanded. He sucked harder, but not too hard.

The harder he sucked, the harder his dick got. His dick was beating between his thighs, and her pussy was on fire.

Lexxy began tugging at her dress, pulling it up over her thighs. When she got to her stomach, Cocaine stopped sucking on her nipples and started kissing down her arms, down her sides, and then down her stomach.

He stopped to peek at the blue lace thong panties she wore, and he ripped them off. As soon as he saw them, something inside of them changed. He saw Lexxy as an innocent type of woman, but those naughty lace panties said otherwise. He was going to show her what looking sexy like that would get her.

When her panties were ripped away from her body, she gasped, shocked that he'd done that, but she liked it.

He looked at her glistening pussy, and it was already shining. It was shaved, so she was so pretty below, looking like two chocolate melons, separated by an opening.

He went to work sucking on her pussy lips, licking all the juices off of them. She had her fingers in his hair, trying not to scratch the shit out of him because of how good it was feeling. Lucky rarely gave her head, so this had her going crazy.

Cocaine opened up her pussy, and her clit was so fat and pink. He knew the way he was going to lick it was going to have her cumming everywhere, and he wanted that shit all over his face.

He started teasing her clit with his tongue, licking slowly, up and down. Making her clit and body jump every time he licked it.

"Mmm....Cocaine!" she screamed. He put his hand on her mouth because he didn't want them to wake Denise. But that just made Lexxy suck Cocaine's fingers, and if she sucked dick anything like she sucked his fingers, ooh wee, it was going to be a problem, the good kind.

Her breathing sped up, and she was about to cum everywhere when she tried to get off the bed. She managed to flip all the way over on her belly, and that was the wrong thing to do. Cocaine had a good look at her pussy from the back, and now he knew that was where he belonged. He pulled her ass back down the bed, and she yelped, then giggled.

He pulled his pants down just enough to get his rock hard dick out of his pants, and then he slid it in her. She was so wet and so tight, Cocaine thought he would bust as soon as he slid in.

"So you wanna run from me?" he asked loudly.

"No!" she screamed.

"Yeah, you do, but I'm 'bout to give you somethin' to run from."

Cocaine went deep inside of her, and she almost threw up the dick was so big. She was almost flying to the top of the pillows his dick was going so far inside of her. After the first ten strokes, she finally started to relax, and she could enjoy it.

Cocaine was going strong, beating her from the back like his life depended on it. Like she was the last woman he was going to ever fuck again.

"Cocaine! Oh, my…mmm fuck me harder!"

He didn't know if he should go any further. He didn't want her bleeding, and he didn't want to hurt her, but Cocaine assumed she knew her own limits, so he did what she wanted.

Cocaine slammed into her, and each time, she screamed. There was no doubt that Denise was definitely awake now.

"Mmm…Lexxy…you…gon'…be…my…bitch!"

"Yes! Whatever you say!"

Cocaine loved the way women would say anything during sex, but he wanted to hear that. He knew that would make his orgasm that much better.

"Where you want me to cum at, baby?" he asked as he kept slamming against her.

She turned around and opened her mouth. Lexxy was a nasty bitch, but she'd never been one for someone she didn't really know. But this was turning out to be everything. She wanted to try something different, and she was feeling adventurous. On top of that, she was halfway delirious from all the dick she'd gotten. She would've given away the family secrets in that moment if he would've asked.

Cocaine couldn't wait to see his cum dripping from her mouth because he just knew she wasn't going to swallow. He dipped his dick into her mouth, and when she tasted her juices, she started going crazy sucking his dick. She always wondered what she tasted like on someone else, and now she knew. She was sucking his dick, sucking her juices, and Cocaine's legs began to tense up. He was about to spill his seed into her mouth, and she knew it. She pushed his dick as far down her throat as it would go, and he couldn't help it, he came, and she swallowed every drop of his creamy cum.

Cocaine couldn't believe it, and neither could Lexxy. It was like she had been in a trance until that moment. She watched Cocaine go to the bathroom, and when he came back out, he had a warm rag for them both. He wiped her pussy, and she jumped when the water touched her clit. She was super sensitive.

Lexxy wiped off his dick and balls, and then she put their washcloths in her dirty clothes hamper. Lexxy was embarrassed about what she had just done. Cocaine could see it on her face, but he wanted her to know it was nothing wrong with the way she was acting or what she had done. She scooted back up on the bed and threw the cover over her body.

"Baby, what you hidin' for? You a grown ass woman, and if you wanna fuck and be nasty, ain't shit wrong with that. Now scoot over and move them covers, girl. A nigga needs a nap."

She opened her eyes wide as Cocaine took off his clothes and stripped down to his boxers to get in her bed. He opened his arm and let her in, cradling her like a baby.

Before he closed his eyes and went to sleep, he told Lexxy he wasn't going anywhere. Now, she wasn't going to be able to get rid of him, and he meant that shit. Now that he had that good ass pussy, he would murder behind it…literally.

CHAPTER 15

Seven months later…

Cocaine and Lexxy were a regular couple, as happy as any couple could be. Lexxy felt comfortable and confident in knowing that Cocaine wasn't going anywhere and that he was fully committed to her. He proposed to her all the time, sometimes with different rings, and she said no every time. She wasn't ready to get married just yet, and she wanted to wait, especially with her going back to school to get the proper licensure to become a surgeon.

Cocaine ended up staying at Lexxy's house most nights because they couldn't stand being away from one another. Cocaine often invited her to stay at his house, but she declined because she was afraid that was the mistake she made with Lucky. She knew if she went to his place and saw where he slept at night, she was going to want to move in with him, and she didn't want to kill a good thing, not if she didn't have to.

Lexxy had been working full time at the hospital for the last several months, and she loved her job. She'd delivered over a dozen babies and had regular patients. She loved the chaos of the emergency room, something about it gave her an adrenaline rush, and she loved that feeling. It never seemed to get old.

Every Wednesday, Cocaine came and had lunch with Lexxy at the hospital. It was her only day where she could get away for lunch for some reason, and she always spent it with Cocaine.

Cocaine walked through the hospital proudly and boldly. He loved telling people his woman was a doctor. Sometimes he found himself just telling random people because he didn't fuck with anybody. Since he and Lexxy had been together, he'd put getting his revenge on hold for a minute so he could spend some time with his woman. He wasn't letting it go; he was just briefly pausing on it for now so he could be with Lexxy.

In one hand, he had food, and in the other, he was carrying flowers for his lady. She smiled when she saw him and put her clipboard down on the counter.

"Hi, daddy! How's your day?"

"Better now that I'm here with you. I went to the bank earlier, then got food and flowers for you."

"The bank?" she asked as they began walking to her office in the hospital.

"Yeah. I had to pick up my money. I still make money back home, baby."

"I mean, I figured that, but I didn't think you got that money through the bank."

"What? 'Cuz I'm a street nigga, I can't have a bank account?"

"No, that's not what I mean. I've never seen you with a debit card in the seven months we've been together. I've been through your wallet a dozen times."

"You've been through my wallet?"

"Hell yeah, nigga. I got to know who I'm laying with at night."

Lexxy opened her door, so they could walk in and closed the door behind them.

"I'ma show you who you layin' wit' at night, alright."

He put their food down in the chair, and Lexxy knocked her keyboard off her desk. Thank God the actual computer was on the other side, or that shit would've gone on the floor too. Cocaine pulled down her scrubs, and he pulled his pants down. He licked his fingers and rubbed the head of his dick, then he rubbed it across her clit. She was wet and ready for him, and he didn't want to wait another minute.

She wrapped her legs around his waist as he entered her. The harder he thrust, the further down on the desk her back went. She was eventually laying all the way back on her desk, and Cocaine was on top of her, tearing her guts up. Lexxy had been working so many shifts at the hospital lately, she'd hardly been home, and Cocaine was missing his pussy. He didn't give a fuck; today he was gon' feel her insides.

"You know who you layin' wit', baby?"

"No! Show me, show me!"

Cocaine rammed into her pussy harder each time, her pussy farting on his dick, and her juices flying all over the place.

Cocaine was about to cum, and he made it a habit to not cum inside of her, not because he didn't want to, but because he didn't want to make Lexxy feel uncomfortable. When she grabbed his ass and pushed him into her, he knew she wanted to feel his cum, so he went harder and faster, and his cum flew out of his body like an airplane during take off.

He breathed heavily on top of her, resting his head on her. He'd exhausted all of his energy, and now he needed to eat that food he brought.

Cocaine rolled off of her and pulled up his pants and helped Lexxy off the desk. He picked up her keyboard and put it back on the desk.

"So, tell me about your day, baby. What's happened so far?"

"Well, I delivered a baby early this morning, but other than that, and a coughing kid, the day has been pretty light."

"Good. You gettin' off on time tonight, baby? I ain't feelin' sleepin' without you."

"Yes, baby. Remember I get off early today so that I can go to class, and then I'll be home around seven."

Cocaine had fallen in love with Lexxy, and he'd told her many times. Often at night, he had nightmares, but when he slept beside Lexxy, he only dreamed of her. It helped to keep his demons at bay.

"I love you, Lexxy."

"I love you too, Coco."

Cocaine looked up in surprise. No one had ever called him that but his father. When she said it, it didn't seem out of place; it sounded like it was always right, like it was something she'd always said.

"What?" she asked, somewhat confused by the look on his face.

Before he could answer, her phone was ringing.

"Hold on, baby."

She answered the phone, forgetting to look at the Caller ID.

"Hello?"

"Hello, princess. How's work?"

It was her father, and she knew if she didn't ask him what he wanted, he would stay on the phone for the next hour, and her break would be over.

"It's fine, Daddy, what's up?"

"I wanted to invite you and that boyfriend of yours over for dinner. Tomorrow good?"

There was an eerie silence on both ends of the phone. Lexxy didn't know if she wanted to have dinner with her father and her boyfriend, and she didn't know if Cocaine would want to either. Cocaine wasn't the type she would normally bring around, and she knew how his personality was. He was very strong minded and even more opinionated, so he'd definitely let her know if he wanted to go or not.

"Uhm…I'll need to ask him first to see what his plans are."

"Ok, ask him and call me back."

"No need, he's right here, hold on, Daddy."

She figured it would be best to go ahead and get it out of the way, so there wouldn't be a later discussion about it. Lexxy also realized this was her father testing her relationship; she just hoped neither shen or Cocaine would fail.

Lexxy proceeded to ask Cocaine what he thought about the dinner, and he shook his head yes. He couldn't wait to meet Lexxy's people. He wondered if he was ever going to get the chance to since Lucky didn't.

"He said that's fine, Daddy."

"Ok, see you tomorrow at five, dinner time hasn't changed."

"Yes, sir."

Lexxy hung up the phone and continued her lunch/work date with Cocaine. Though she didn't say anything, she was a bit nervous. No, nervous wasn't the right word. She knew how her father could be, and she just hoped he didn't embarrass her or ruin it for her. She loved Cocaine, and she wanted to make him happy and feel welcomed. She just hoped her father didn't fuck this up for her. He had a way of making shit turn out wrong, but she couldn't let that happen with Cocaine. She was finally happy, and she intended to stay that way.

CHAPTER 16

"Wait, you're going where?" Denise asked as she paced the room.

Lexxy had quit working at the diner and was at home less and less. The only time she saw Denise was in passing or right when she came home before Lexxy was about to leave for work or school. She wasn't able to tell Denise that she was going to be eating dinner at her daddy's house with Cocaine 'til the day of, and Denise was surprised her daddy even extended the invitation.

"Lawd, did you tell Cocaine to be on his best behavior, bitch? Maybe I need to call out so I can go with you for just in case."

"No, girl. He's just gon' have to accept the fact that I'm getting serious with somebody, and everybody don't want our money. Most people don't even care about that shit, and besides, Cocaine has his own money. He don't need mine!"

"I know that's right. Now, while you talkin' all that big girl shit, I hope you keep that same attitude when you see him. Go get 'em, tiger!"

Lexxy frowned at Denise, but she was right. Lexxy was talking shit now, but what she would do when she got in front of her father, could be a different story. She didn't want to disrespect her father, but she was an adult, and he needed to show her the respect she deserved. He needed to know that, because she was an adult. Regardless of what he wanted, it wasn't up to him. She didn't leave Lucky even though her parents had told her to, and no matter what he said about Cocaine, she wasn't going to leave him either.

Cocaine wasn't as clean cut as Lucky, nor was he a legitimate worker, but that shouldn't have mattered. Cocaine was all she wanted and needed, and this was the real deal.

When Cocaine came to pick her up, she had a hard time getting her feet out the door. She wanted to hurry and get outside, but she was afraid. She was scared if she showed up for this dinner, what it would do to her relationship. She didn't want her father to dislike Cocaine or vice versa. He told her that he'd never really dated anyone and that this was his first real relationship, so he didn't know the protocol for meeting parents, especially parents who were still together and were active parts of their daughter's life.

After a few minutes of obsessing over the issue, she got over herself and went on outside and got in the car.

"Hello, beautiful," Cocaine said as he leaned over and kissed her.

"Hi, baby. You want me to drive?"

"Nah, show me how to get there."

Lexxy gave him directions to the house, and when they reached the driveway, they had to drive down it for miles and miles.

"Damn, baby, we gettin' any closer to the house? We been in the car for almost an hour!"

"I told you they lived kind of far."

"Nah, the house wasn't that far, this driveway is far. Got damn!"

Lexxy laughed and put her hand on Cocaine's leg. He continued driving, and finally, literally five miles later, a very large yard appeared with a white fence around it. It looked like the perfect dream house for the most part. Well, he couldn't see the house just yet.

As they continued driving, the workers waved at Lexxy, and she waved back. The only people who knew about this back entrance were family and security. When they came to the back gate, there was a man inside of a fenced-in port.

"Hey, Lexxy, you plus one?"

"Yes sir, how are the kids?" Lexxy asked the man who was about to let them in the gate. Her father had the same people working for him for most of her life.

"They're great. You know Sarah just went off to college."

"Sarah's in school? Where?"

"Georgia Tech."

"Oh, I'll have to send her something. Get the information and give it to my dad, please. It was good to see you!"

Lexxy stuck her hand out the window and waved goodbye. Cocaine loved that about her. She was so down to earth, and she was smart. Her personality was so contagious; he loved being around her.

As they approached the house, it was smaller than

what Cocaine thought it would be. It wasn't nearly as big as the land.

"Anti-climactic, huh?" Lexxy asked as she noticed Cocaine's face change.

"Kind of, but that ain't my business. I mean, the top of the house seems bigger than the rest of the actual house."

"We're having dinner in the guest house because Mommy is having the big house renovated. Plus, Daddy won't ever admit it, but he likes the guest house better."

"Mmm…must be nice. What exactly did you say your father did?"

"I didn't…."

Cocaine nodded his head and figured her father must've been a black executive of some sort because he had too much money and way too much damn land.

As they pulled up to the house, Lexxy noticed Wild Bill standing on the porch waiting for her to get out of the car. She got out and ran up the stairs and hugged her uncle.

"'Hey, baby girl. Glad to see you could make it."

"Of course. What choice did I really have?"

"I guess you didn't have one, not really. Hey, Cocaine. Leave your keys in the car, they'll park it for you," Wild Bill said as he used one hand to point over to the valet station.

Cocaine's eyes got big, and he was surprised. Who the fuck had valet at their house?

"How you doin', though, young buck?" Wild Bill asked Cocaine.

"I'm good, old head. Anything you can tell me about her pops to get me in good?"

"SSShhhiiittt.....no matter what you say, it's gon' be wrong. Just face that, and you'll be ok. Accept defeat before it happens."

"Unc!" Lexxy said as she lightly tapped Wild Bill.

"I'm just sayin'." Wild Bill shrugged his shoulders because shit, he wasn't lying.

Wild Bill walked them in the house, and it was simple but elegant. The décor was red and brown, there was a chandelier above their heads illuminated in bright lights, and the dining room, which was directly to the right, was decorated with place settings and beautiful tableware.

"Where's Daddy?" Lexxy asked Wild Bill.

"I'll go get him, hold on."

Lexxy figured she'd follow him so she could give him a talk. She didn't want him saying anything stupid if she could help it.

"Stay right here, baby. I'll be right back."

Lexxy gave Cocaine a kiss that lingered on a bit longer than Wild Bill would've liked. He coughed, letting Lexxy know it was time to pull away, and she continued following him. She didn't get too far before her father was coming out of his study.

"Baby girl! Look at you, beautiful!"

"Daddy!"

Even though Lexxy's father irritated her, and he could do the most sometimes, she loved him as any girl loves her father. She was still like a child around him most of the time. She hugged him tightly, taking in his scent.

"Where's that boyfriend of yours?" he asked her.

"Come on, I'll show you."

Lexxy and her father took a few steps around the corner, and when Cocaine looked up, he saw Lexxy, and she was glowing. She was happy to be here with her dad, and he was happy that she was happy. She often complained about how overbearing he could be, but what father wasn't, especially over his daughter?

"Cocaine, this is my dad, Dutch. Daddy, this is Cocaine."

Cocaine looked up and into Lexxy's father's eyes with his hand stretched out. He went to shake his hand, but then a wave of bloodlust washed over him. Though the man's skin had had some type of surgery to remove it, he could tell by the scar he had on his face; he knew this man! The gorilla tattoo was no longer there, but he knew it was him, not to mention, he knew the name. How could this happen to him? Dutch was Lexxy's father?

As badly as he wanted to ask questions, he was always taught to shoot first and ask questions later.

He reached into the small of his shirt with a smile on his face, pushed the safety off, pulled the hammer back, and fired twice.

Finally, he had gotten his revenge; he could go on with his life. Sure, he'd probably lose Lexxy, which he hoped he wouldn't because he had explained to her everything. He'd told her everything about how his father was killed, and she didn't know her father was a monster.

Her father fell to the ground, and it was like Cocaine had tunnel vision, he couldn't see anything else going on around him. Wild Bill was on the ground, next to Dutch, but where was Lexxy? He looked on the ground, and there she was, covered in blood.

"Baby? Baby?" Cocaine said as he got down on the floor.

There was blood everywhere, leaking toward him... This was not the way he expected this dinner to turn out, and his revenge was not turning out to be so sweet after all...

"Baby, baby, please get up. Lexxy, come on, baby. I'm sorry, please!" Cocaine screamed as he lie on top of her body, begging her to get up. She had her eyes wide open, stuck with terror. Blood seeped out of the holes in her body. No matter how much Cocaine tried, he couldn't plug the wounds; he couldn't stop the bleeding.

"Get this nigga out of here now, Bill!" Dutch yelled as he placed his hands behind Lexxy's hand, trying to hold her head up.

"'N-no, daddy. C-Co-Cocaine…" Lexxy said through gurgled blood. She didn't want Cocaine to leave. Even though her life was about to be cut short, she didn't want him to leave, and she knew what would happen to him if she didn't save him. She knew what Wild Bill was capable of and what he had done in the past. He wouldn't hesitate if it weren't for her, and she was thankful that she was able to speak in that moment.

It was in that moment that Cocaine felt he had to tell the truth about what was going on. Not that he'd lied because everything was happening so fast.

"Baby, baby, I'm sorry, I'm so sorry. I just lost it. Your father…he killed my father. He's the gorilla faced man," Cocaine confessed, wishing that it weren't true.

Lexxy knew how much pain this caused him. She knew how he wanted to get revenge, and she wanted him to get some type of solace, but she never thought she'd have anything to do with it.

Dutch looked at Cocaine trying to figure out what he was talking about. He hadn't killed anyone in years, but he'd killed a lot of men, so he could've been talking about anyone.

"Who was your pops, Cocaine?" Wild Bill asked, curiosity swirling around him.

"Juaqeen, Juaqeen Blackwood."

Wild Bill's eyes got wide, and he looked at Dutch, who was convulsing in laughter, but his laughter was interrupted by Lexxy who was coughing up blood.

Cocaine wasn't the type to cry. The last time he shed a tear was the day his father died, and he hadn't dropped one since, but that fact didn't stop the water from rushing from his eyes like he was a small child again. He loved Lexxy, and he would kill her father for sure if she died. There would be no going back or taking it back because it was his fault in the first damn place. If he hadn't have killed his father, he would've never even been in Tennessee, and if he wasn't the killer, he would have never had to put him out of his fucking misery, but Lexxy just got in the way. He wasn't even paying attention. His mind only saw red when he appeared. He wanted to take that nigga out and all costs, so he thought. He thought he was ready to give it all up for the revenge he sought, but seeing Lexxy go down made him realize he was willing to lose it all except Lexxy.

Wild Bill stood off to the side, calling their private

doctor. They couldn't afford a hospital situation. Lexxy had already burnt her house down, and now a gunshot wound? No, that would not fly well with the NPD, even though Dutch had them wrapped tightly, there were some things money couldn't buy, and that was a blind eye from the Feds.

He said he would be there shortly. Luckily for them, he lived on the outskirts of the property. They pretty much paid him to not have a life in case emergencies like this arose. He instructed them not to move her, but to try and keep her comfortable.

Twenty minutes later, the doctor burst through the door, walking in with a heavy, black leather bag. He threw his bag down and went into the kitchen to scrub up. As he stood in the kitchen, he wondered what the hell happened, but he didn't have time for specifics. He needed to get in there and work on Lexxy. As he passed her when he initially came in the house, he not only saw the blood, but he could smell it, and it was reeking the house up.

As he finished scrubbing his hands, he called out from the kitchen the things he needed, and Wild Bill and Dutch ran around the house like mad men trying to gather the things necessary to help her.

Doctor Logan got on the floor, assessing the situation. One bullet had gone straight through her kidney, and another had gone through her shoulder, and it was stuck directly between her shoulder blade. If she had any chance of living, he had to somehow manage the bleeding from her kidney and get the bullet out of her shoulder, but that would be impossible without being in an actual hospital.

"She's gonna have to go to the hospital. The blood is turning dark, and she's got blood rushing from her mouth, which means she's bleeding internally. I can probably stop the bleeding for now, but she won't make it if she doesn't get to the hospital," Doctor Logan spoke honestly.

He'd known Lexxy for most of her life. He was her pediatrician as a child and had been their family's doctor forever. Seeing her in this predicament was not only sad, but it was tragic.

Wild Bill pulled out his phone, preparing to call the ambulance when Dutch held his hand up.

"We've gotta take her. Waiting for the ambulance will take too long, and they'll have a hard time getting all the way back here. Bill, go get the car, and I'll bring her outside."

"No, I will," Cocaine said as he slid his hands underneath Lexxy and hoisted her up into his arms.

There was no time to argue; they had to focus on saving Lexxy.

Seconds later, Bill was whipping his car into the front of the house, running from the driver's side to the back of the car and ripping the door open for Lexxy and Cocaine.

Slowly and steadily, Cocaine lay Lexxy in the backseat, and he slid in with her. Somewhere between the doctor coming in the house and her getting in the car, she had blacked out. Her eyes were now closed, and her breathing was very shallow.

Dutch flew out of the house and jumped in the car.

Wild Bill jet through the city streets, racing through traffic trying to get Lexxy to the hospital before it was too late. Doctor Logan made it clear what they were facing, and Wild Bill would be damned if he let something bad happen to his niece.

Cocaine held Lexxy in his arms, kissing her, rubbing his hands over her face. For the first time since his father died, he felt fear, real fear. He would die if he lost Lexxy. His life wouldn't even be worth living, and the fact that he misfired had his mind fucked up. He thought for sure he'd shot Dutch. His mind was racing so fast, he forgot about Lexxy even being there. How could he be so reckless, so careless? That just wasn't like him in all honesty. Cocaine was careful, strategic even, so for this to have happened like this, he wanted to die right along with Lexxy.

He could smell her body—it was the worst smell he'd ever encountered. He'd been around dead bodies, and even dying bodies, but never long enough to smell them, or maybe he'd never paid attention before, but Lexxy was his woman, his rib, and she was slipping away. Her rich chocolate skin was fading to a stale dark brown. She was still beautiful in his eyes, but he could feel her essence slipping away.

While they were in the car, Dutch kept a watch on Lexxy and Cocaine through the rearview mirror. He was so angry with Cocaine, but now wasn't the time to react, though he had plenty to say and so much he wanted to do to Cocaine. He'd kill him the same way he killed his father. He felt no remorse for what he did. Why should he? He killed him to steal what he felt was rightfully his; unfortunately, Cocaine just happened to be there, but if he would've known that he was there, he would've killed him that day too. They could've gone on to the after life together since it was so important for Cocaine to avenge his father's death.

They arrived at the hospital, right in the front loop. Cocaine carefully removed his hands and leg from underneath Lexxy's head as Wild Bill came around the side to open the door. Dutch ran into the hospital, yelling, his voice cracking.

"My daughter's been shot! Get out here and help her!"

Several nurses ran outside pushing a gurney. The nurses who weren't assisting with the gurney were trying to remove Lexxy from the car so they could get her into the hospital. Once she was secure, they wheeled her inside, and a doctor came around the side with his flashlight, checking her eyes, and asking what happened.

Dutch gave them the details, and Cocaine held her hand tightly, squeezing her. Hoping she'd be ok.

"I'm sorry, sir, you have to let her go so we can work on her," the young doctor said, his lips kindly turning up into a smile.

Cocaine kissed her hand like it was the last time he'd ever see her, then he bent down and whispered into her ear.

"I love you so much, baby. I don't care if you never forgive me; you gotta live through this shit. I rather you live and be mad at me, then die and never get to properly hate me. Come back to me, baby."

A few hours later, the doctor still hadn't come out with any news about Lexxy. No one had any information available to give to Cocaine, who was literally misty eyed, Dutch who was cursing the entire nursing staff out, and Wild Bill who could've pulled the floor up with how much he was pacing back and forth.

Dutch was headed into another cursing fit when the doors of the hospital flew open, and in walked an older, more polished version of Lexxy. Though she was fair skinned, it couldn't be denied that she was Lexxy's mother. Their hair, bone structure, smile, and even body shapes were the same. Dutch had called Junie once Lexxy went into surgery. He didn't want Lexxy to die before Junie had a chance to say goodbye or know what was going on if it got that far. She'd definitely never forgive him, and by the way she sounded on the phone, he could already tell there would be hell to pay when she came in. He did his best to explain to her what happened on the phone, but she wasn't trying to hear it. She had two things on her mind, and Dutch was not one of them. The first, was how her baby was doing and if they'd heard anything; the second was Cocaine. She was mad that her daughter was caught in the crossfire, but she was angrier with her husband for leaving behind such tragedy that it could potentially come back to bite them, and she always knew it would, though she didn't think it would be this. She didn't even know exactly what this was.

Dutch rose to greet his wife, and she put her French

manicured hand in his face, curving whatever he was going to say.

She nodded at Wild Bill and went straight over to Cocaine, who had his head in his hands, trying to get himself together. Dopeboys cried too.

"Excuse me, Cocaine?" Junie said as she placed her hand on his shoulder. She felt strange for even calling him that, but she knew all too well how street names became real names, but in Cocaine's case, this was his real name, and he would never change it. It was a name he was proud of because it came from his father.

Cocaine looked up and into Junie's eyes. He knew instantly who she was, and he stood to greet her.

"Y-Yes, ma'am?" he stuttered as he met her gaze. He was so ashamed and embarrassed by what he had done and looking at Junie was driving him crazy. He kept thinking about how she looked just like Lexxy and hoped she'd make it long enough to grow as old as her mother.

"Come over here with me, son, let me talk to you," she said as she reached out for his hand. He grabbed it, hoping she wasn't leading him to his death, at least not without him being able to say goodbye to Lexxy first.

"Now you listen to me, what you did has brought on consequences that none of us are willing to face, so you better hope with everything in you that my baby pulls through, but I understand why you did it. Hell, I'd try to kill his ass too. I'm so sorry for the loss of your father, even more so at the hands of my stupid ass husband. I can only imagine how you feel, and if you're as important to Lexxy as she tells me you are, then you're family, and we don't condemn family; we console them. Give me a hug, baby."

Junie wrapped her arms around Cocaine, feeling sorry for him. She had lost her father at an early age, and the pain never really went away. She was always hurting about it, on his birthday, on her birthday, any time there was a special event or something amazing was happening. It never got any easier, and she knew that, and from what Lexxy told her, Cocaine didn't have a mother, so she knew he probably grew up hard.

Cocaine wasn't used to being treated so kindly, or like he mattered really to anyone but Lexxy. How was it even possible that Cocaine had fucked up so bad, yet her mother, the person who gave birth to her was being so understanding? A part of Cocaine wanted to believe it was a trick of some sort, but it wasn't. Junie truly felt sorry for him.

As Junie held Cocaine in her arms, he wondered if this was what it was like to have the redeeming love of a mother, and he wished he knew his mother. He wished he would've been given the chance to meet her before she passed away, but Junie was helping to soften that spot in his heart that he thought he'd long ago closed off to women, her and Lexxy. He now held a soft spot for Lexxy and her mother, and he realized why it was so easy to fall for Lexxy; she was just like her mother, but what Cocaine didn't understand was how Dutch was able to get such a wonderful woman, that he clearly didn't deserve.

After several moments of Junie's embrace, Cocaine

finally pulled away and spoke. "I'm so sorry. I'm…I'm so sorry."

"Shh…don't you apologize. It isn't your fault. It's Dutch's fault. Things were never supposed to be this way. I was groomed for the street life, but that doesn't mean it gets any easier, especially when your husband won't tell you the truth. Give me one moment to speak with my husband."

Junie walked away from Cocaine to scold Dutch. She was mad at Dutch not because this happened, but the why it happened. It was his fault.

Dutch loved Junie; he always had. He'd loved her since before she even knew who he was, and it pained him for her to be upset, but he couldn't do anything about it. He knew whatever she was about to say was about to burn.

"Baby, before you say anything…"

"Nope, shut the fuck up, Dutch. I don't even want to hear it. I told you that one fucking day, one dark, sad fucking day, some shit was going to come back and bite us, and I can only imagine how you reacted to being told this was an attempt on your life because of some old dirt you did. You're not funny! This shit is not funny! How would you feel if this happened to Lexxy? If you were taken from her, and she retaliated? Never mind, don't answer that, your answer is only going to piss me the fuck off! We'll talk about this later, but not right now. Have they said anything about our baby?"

Junie had given him an earful, and she wasn't done; she was just taking a break.

"They haven't said anything yet. I've threatened everyone, and still, there's been no news."

"Threatening people doesn't always get the job done. Let me go speak to someone."

Junie rolled her eyes and took a deep breath before turning around to speak to someone at the nurse's station. She needed to be on her p's and q's if she was going to get something accomplished. She wasn't like Dutch. She was rational, and she was good to have in a bad situation. She knew how to keep a cool head and how to get shit done without making them worse. She wished she wouldn't have even left home. She wondered if she could've prevented the situation from happening. Had she been around when this shit was about to pop off, maybe she would've noticed the gun being pulled out, maybe she would've seen the outcome before it happened, but she wasn't there, and she rarely ever was. Junie was a good mother, but she wasn't always there when she probably should've been, but she loved her job. She was able to travel and meet people she'd never dreamed she could've met without her position, but now that she was needed, she was here, and ready to help however she could.

Her baby was in surgery, fighting for her life, and she was just glad that she wasn't going to miss this. Lexxy was grown, but she'd always be her baby.

CHAPTER 18

The black walls around Lexxy seemed to be getting smaller and smaller the longer she stood in place.

Where am I? she asked herself, wondering what was going on. Around her, she heard loud voices, men, women, some with accents, some who spoke perfect English, but she couldn't really see anything.

She felt detached from her body like she wasn't herself, like she was just floating around. Where was she?

Every time she moved, the space she was in got smaller, and soon enough, the place would implode if she took too many steps.

"Hello?" she called out, but there was no one there to answer.

She looked down at herself, and she had on a white hospital gown that was open in the back.

Out of nowhere, she noticed a pinch of light sneaking in, beckoning her to go toward it. She figured anything would be better than the darkness, though she knew there was nothing to fear since the dark was just the absence of light, but she hoped there would be something waiting for her on the other side.

Lexxy walked toward the light, and the pinch became more like a flashlight, and then like a light that had been turned on in a room, and then, it eventually took over the darkness, and it was all white, as bright as the sun.

Lexxy could see two dark figures, and something told her she should walk toward them, to get closer to them.

As she neared the dark figures, she realized she was smack dab in the middle of the two. She squinted her eyes, and she recognized the dread head that stood to her left.

"Lucky, what are you doing here?"

"To be real, I love you too much to let you go. Look over there, that nigga ain't me. We got too much time invested, beautiful."

Lexxy thought about it and realized Lucky was right. They had spent so much time together, and she truly knew him, but did she really wanna run back to him just because she had feelings for him that were dying now because of Cocaine?

She looked to her left and saw Lucky, and then back to her right and saw Cocaine. He was the other shadowy figure. Was she dreaming? She pinched herself to see for sure, but she could feel it, so this wasn't a dream…what was it? What was she going to do?

"Come over here with me...I love you," she heard Lucky's voice call back out to her, but the closer she got to Lucky, the further she got from Cocaine.

Lexxy took Lucky's hands and followed him, slowly and hesitantly, but she went with him nonetheless.

Every few seconds, she kept turning back to look at Cocaine, to see what he was doing, and he was chasing after her with his hands out, longing for her even, she could tell by the face he was making.

"Lucky, where are we?" she asked him, curious as to what was going on.

"I gotta show you something, baby, come on."

Suddenly, Lexxy's feet weren't moving. She was planted firmly to the ground, and she couldn't move. She turned around and saw Cocaine getting closer. Lucky tugged on her hand, trying to pull her out of the place she was in.

"Come on, baby, we gotta go, we gotta go now!" Lucky said, and then his eyes turned starch white, and his body became hazy.

"No!" She snatched away from him, and instantly, she was able to move her feet again.

She remembered what happened between the two of them. She loved Lucky, and a love like that was hard to kill, but she was madly and hopelessly in love with Cocaine, and there was no way she was going to choose Lucky over him, or was she?

Cocaine's bright, white smile blasted in her direction, covering and consuming her with the love they shared, and it was like bathing in sunshine. She knew what she had to do. She took one last look at Lucky and gave him an endearing smile. She would love him for the rest of her life, but she couldn't keep sharing her heart with a man who didn't deserve it, and the man who owned it.

Cocaine opened his arms wide, waiting for her to jump in them, and just before she got to him…everything went dark again, stealing the light from around her love.

When Denise got the call that Lexxy was in the hospital once again, her heart dropped. How did her best friend keep finding herself in these situations? She had no idea, but she couldn't get herself together enough to go see her. She was trying so hard to stay calm and keep a cool head, but that was what Lexxy normally did for her. She was the ice to her fire, and without her, she would surely lose all of her senses.

After hanging up with Wild Bill, she lie on her bed, trying to figure it all out. How could this have happened to Lexxy, her sweet, beautiful Lexxy? She had no one to talk to because she was anti-social, so she took to the only place she knew people would be able to comfort her enough to calm down. She knew she would be no good to anyone at the hospital if she was there having a fit, and she didn't want to do that, not to Lexxy.

She pulled up her Facebook page,and prepared to make a post. She pushed the 'make a post' button, and proceeded to type her message, hoping to gain some sympathy or kind and understanding words.

"How is it that the nicest, best people always get dealt the shittiest hands? Y'all, I'm over here really strugglin', and I feel selfish, but I can't help it. My best friend,

Lexxy was shot, and I know I should be at the hospital, but I can't get my shit together enough to get up and do it. I'm not strong, and I can't find the courage, when she needs me the most. Well, if she even notices I'm not there. I don't know what's going on, there have been no updates, and I can't muster up the nerve to get my ass out of this house. I know I shouldn't be puttin' my business all over Facebook like this, but I don't know what else to do. Please, y'all pray for me before I lose my shit. If I lose my bestie, I won't be no more good. I might as well kill myself too, because it ain't no me without her."

Denise posted the status, and within a minute's time, people were posting, commenting, sending her words of encouragement, prayers, and wishing her and Lexxy well. She sent Wild Bill a text asking if they'd heard anything, and still nothing.

A few hours passed by before Denise was actually able to get up and put on her clothes. She'd been commenting back and forth with some of the people on her post, and she even called Lexxy's boss at the neighboring hospital to let her know what was going on. She didn't want her girl to be without a job or get in any trouble. She didn't know how the hospital world worked, but she knew in the real nine to five world, no call no show meant fired baby.

Denise ran her fingers through her long, fire red Brazillian bundles and threw her hair up in a ponytail. While she was at home, all she had on was a tank top and a pair of black lace panties, and she obviously couldn't go anywhere like that, so she threw on some leggings and grabbed her blue jean jacket and slid into her fuzzy all black Gucci slippers.

She reached for her keys and did a once over of herself in the mirror. In all honesty, she looked like shit. Her eyes were red from crying, and she had circles like racoons parading around her eye rim. She looked awful, and she felt even worse, but she couldn't go out the house looking crazy. She had to be strong for Lexxy because she knew how she was. Her best friend would be more worried about her than she was about herself, and she didn't want to do that to her, not today.

Denise always kept concealer in her bag for emergencies, and this definitely was considered an emergency. She pulled her LA Girl Pro Concealer from her purse that sat underneath the mirror and began dabbing it on her face, covering up the red spots, concealing the pain she held in her face. As she was finishing, she heard a loud knock coming from outside of her door. She turned and looked at it, so annoyed, not knowing who it could be, or what they might want.

She walked over to the door and pulled it open, irritated that she would be held up a second longer.

"Lucky, what the hell are you doing here?" she asked, shocked that he was on her doorstep.

"Yeah….I…I saw your status and figured I'd come over and drive you to the hospital," Lucky said in a low tone as he rubbed his fingers through his luxurious dreads.

Denise folded her arms and shifted her weight to one of her legs.

"No you didn't. You came over here because you

know you can't go to the hospital to see her alone. Why on God's green earth would you think I would take you with me?" she asked honestly. She didn't know if Lucky had fallen and bumped his head, but he was buggin'.

"Look, I ain't come here for all that. Call me crazy, but I feel like her soul is callin' out to me, no joke. I knew something was wrong. I been feelin' it all day. Now look, we sit here arguin' goin' back and forth about what we should or shouldn't do, or you could let me take you to the hospital, since you actin' like you ain't got the strength and shit to move, and we go see our friend together. I still love Lexxy. But I just wanna be there for her as a friend. I don't want no problems."

Denise thought about it, and she really wasn't in any condition to drive, even if she wanted to be, and she hated Lucky for what he did to Lexxy, but this could be the last time any of them saw her, and she didn't want to take away that for him. She could only imagine how he would feel if he didn't get the chance to. She just hoped Cocaine would forgive her and that Lexxy wouldn't be upset.

"Fine," Denise said as she grabbed her purse, zipped it up, and got her house keys.

Lucky played no games getting through the city of Nashville's streets. He had one thing on his mind, and that was Lexxy. Though they had been broken up for some time, he didn't care. He loved her, and he always would. Not even God himself could remove that type of love from him. He wanted to be there for her, to see her. His soul was tied to hers in so many ways, and he knew some shit was off about the day. He'd literally been having the bubble guts all day, and it was more than just not feeling well, it was something wrong, and as soon as he saw Denise's Facebook status, he often crept on her page to see pictures of Lexxy since she blocked him, he kissed his new girlfriend and his son goodbye and left the house. There was no question about where he needed to be. He needed to see her, just to make sure he got the chance to apologize, and if nothing else, to tell her how he loved her truly, and how he would miss her.

He didn't know the full extent of the situation; he just knew what Denise posted on Facebook, and that sounded bad enough to him, and he wanted to be there for Lexxy, even if she wasn't awake, or severely hurt. He needed to do this for himself. The way they ended things, and then seeing each other at the mall, it made it almost impossible to fix what the problem was, and Lucky promised himself if she made it out of this, he would do everything he could to remedy the problems between them because he still loved Lexxy, more than he loved anyone, and she was still the most important person in the world to him, even if she didn't know it.

Lucky whipped into the parking garage of the hospital and got a ticket from the ticket booth for parking. He didn't give a damn how much this shit was going to cost, he would pay it no matter what it was when he left, and hospital parking could be a bitch, but that wasn't important now.

Denise got out of the passenger's side of the car as Lucky hopped out, both feet on the ground, and they both slammed their doors behind them, running into the hospital. They figured they'd both wasted enough time waiting and praying and crying trying to gather the moxie to even go. They didn't know if they even had another moment to spare.

They burst into the hospital, wind blowing off of them as the automatic doors flew open to let them in. As soon as they arrived, they ran straight into Dutch and Junie, and Denise saw Cocaine waiting in a chair with his hands over his head.

"Denise, oh, sweetheart, come here," Junie said as she opened her arms. Denise had been ok. She promised herself she wasn't going to cry. She promised herself that she would hold it together, but how could she? Lexxy was more than a friend; she was like a sister, and she needed to know she was ok.

Tears slid down her face as Junie held her.

"Any news?" Denise asked as she looked at Lucky who was standing off to the side, ear hustling.

Junie noticed what she was doing, and she turned around to look at the gentleman she was staring at.

"Well, she's out of surgery. She isn't completely out of the woods yet. They were able to remove the bullets, but it caused severe damage to one of her kidneys. For now, we're still running tests."

"Can we see her?" Denise asked, and the doctor, who seemed to be invisible appeared out of nowhere.

"Hello, who do we have here?" the doctor asked as he looked at Denise and Lucky.

"This is Denise, Lexxy's best friend, her boyfriend, Cocaine, and this young man," she said as Lucky got closer, "is Lucky. The ex," she whispered as she held her hand up against her mouth. Cocaine rose from his seat and made his way over to where they were.

He was mad that Lucky was there, but he didn't give a shit, at least not then.

"Can we see her?" Cocaine asked as he stared Lucky down, letting him know this was his territory and he had no business being there.

"Yes, but just for a few minutes, and I suggest you go in two at a time, that way she can spend an equal amount of time with everyone. She isn't awake though, the last time I checked, but sure, go ahead and go in," the doctor instructed.

Cocaine began walking toward the door, and Dutch, who until that moment had been very quiet, finally spoke up.

"I don't know what you think you're doing, but her mother and I will be the first to go in."

"No, I'm going in first. I need to see her. You've had a lifetime with her, and because of you, my time with her has possibly been cut short."

Dutch balled his hand up and raised his fist. Junie saw what was about to happen, and she grabbed him, giving him a stern look. It was about to get real in this hospital if someone didn't diffuse the situation.

CHAPTER 20

"Dutch, have you lost your motherfucking mind?" Junie asked as she grabbed him.

"Nah, he's clearly lost his damn mind! She's my child, and I should see her first."

Junie shook her head. She couldn't believe Dutch was acting this way. This was a side of him she hadn't seen in so long, she almost forgot it existed. When they were younger, she found his selfishness almost exciting. She always saw him as ambitious and fun, but now that they were older, the shit wasn't cute, and she didn't like it.

"If I, the person who gave birth to her didn't rush to go in, then what the fuck is wrong with you? Get Cocaine, go on in, baby. Go ahead."

Dutch tried to rush past her, and she got in front of him. Junie wasn't a large woman, but she wasn't a small woman either, and she wasn't going to tolerate the disrespect from her husband, not after all he'd done.

"Dutch, so help me God, if you don't calm the fuck down, I'll punch you the fuck out myself. After all, this shit is your fault! You did this. This mayhem and chaos, that was you, nigga. Now chill out, or you can fucking leave! Cocaine, you go ahead and go in, baby," Junie said over her shoulder.

Dutch yanked away from Junie, and he turned around, storming out of the hospital. As always, he was throwing a fit. He could be such a brat and a baby, and today was not the day for him to be having one of his tantrums.

Denise went toward the door, following after Cocaine, but when the door opened, she stopped. Her heart was pounding out of her chest, and her stomach was turning, wrenching with fear. She looked away for a moment to try and gather her thoughts and herself, and she couldn't control the feeling her stomach was giving off. She threw up on the floor, everywhere.

"Oh, no!" Junie ran over to Denise, trying to pull her hair out of her way. She was releasing all of the fear and anxiety she felt on the floor. Lucky noticed she looked a little pale, but who wasn't? They were all looking a bit peak-ish, but he felt like that was his opportunity to go in with Cocaine, and he didn't give a damn what Cocaine had to say about it. He was going to see the love of his life.

As he entered the room, Cocaine looked up and rolled his eyes. He didn't want to have it out with him like this, but as long as he kept it cool and respected the boundaries that didn't need to be said aloud, it would all be fine.

Cocaine stood to the right side of her bed, holding her hand, apologizing. She wasn't awake, but his spirit told him she could hear him.

Lucky came around the other side, holding her left hand, and he began praying silently, begging God to let her be alright.

Cocaine didn't believe in God, not really. He believed in a creator and a greater purpose for all, but the big man in the sky, he wasn't too keen on him. He didn't understand how a God, the man who created life, could take it in such a cruel manor, but at this point, he was willing to do what it took. He figured when Lucky closed his eyes, that that was what he was doing, so he joined him silently.

Lexxy was surrounded by love and prayer warriors, even if they didn't know the strength in what they were doing.

Lucky ended his prayer first but stayed silent as he saw Cocaine doing the same thing, and as Cocaine said amen, Lexxy's eyes shot open, as if electricity had been pumped through her body.

She inhaled a breath like it was the first breath she'd ever taken, like a newborn babe fresh out of the womb. She looked to her right at her man, and tears welled up in her eyes. This was the person she wanted to see most.

"Baby," she said just above a whisper, just enough for him to hear.

"Lexxy," he replied, putting his head on top of hers, taking in the essence he felt fleeing her body just hours before. He wrapped his arm around her face, admiring her beauty, and a sense of relief washed over him. He hadn't lost his woman to his own stupidity.

"I'm sor—"

"Shh…." She cut him off. In truth, Lexxy wasn't ready to know what was going on. She wanted to enjoy her peace for as long as she could before things started getting weird.

On her left side, she felt something, or someone, tugging at her other hand. Cocaine lifted his head, and she looked to the left and saw Lucky. Now she wondered if she had been dreaming, if this was all just her imagination, but why would she be imagining the same thing twice? That wasn't right.

"Lucky?" she asked, confused as to why he would be in her room and how Cocaine even allowed it. She thought for sure if they were ever this close to each other again while she and Cocaine were together, there would be a problem.

"I came to check on you, of course. Denise made a huge Facebook status about you, and when I saw it....I just had to see how you were," Lucky admitted as his golden hazel eyes sparkled with joy.

Lexxy smiled. She didn't really know what to say, or what would be appropriate to say, so she didn't open her mouth. She turned her head back to look at Cocaine who had a smile on his face the size of the Kool-Aid man, and the door swung open, and in walked the doctor.

"Hello, Lexxy. How are you feeling?" Doctor Graham asked as he came near her bed to check her vital signs.

"I'm ok. Tired and sore, but ok."

"Good. I'm glad to hear it. I wanted to come in and discuss your test results with you. I figured I should discuss them with you in private if you were awake, and since you are..."

"Private? Whatever you need to say, you can say it in front of these two," Lexxy said as she nodded her head in both of their directions. Cocaine didn't like that though.

He didn't want Lucky in there with them, not to hear whatever it was the doctor was about to say, but he knew he had to pick and choose his battles, and he didn't want to upset Lexxy, so he kept quiet.

"Well, after further tests, examinations, and a full x-ray, while we were able to remove the bullets, and stop the bleeding, the lead from the bullet spread to your left kidney and has damaged it beyond repair. We can remove it, but your right kidney will have to work double time to make up for the one that's being removed since you suffered such trauma to your body."

"So, what are you sayin', doc?" Cocaine raised his eyebrows and squeezed Lexxy's hand, while Lucky stood there, trying not to pass out.

"A transplant would be ideal."

"Transplant?" The word seemed almost foreign to Lexxy. Sure, she'd heard it before, but the fact that she was going to need one blew her mind. Her brain instantly went to thinking about those people in the movies who died before they could ever get the transplant they needed.

The doctor saw the horror in her eyes and tried his best to comfort her.

"Let's just try to stay positive. If your family is willing, we could test them to see if they are a match. If so, we can prep them for surgery right away."

"And if not?" Cocaine wasn't prepared to hear the worst about this situation, but he needed to know what was going on for his own sanity. He would give her a foot if he could. If his kidney could save her life, hell, if she needed both, he'd give them to her just so she could live.

He wanted nothing more than for her to be happy, healthy, and of course, alive.

"If not, then she'll go on the donor waiting list, and we'll just have to play it by ear."

Both Cocaine and Lucky looked into the doctor's eyes, and neither of them could believe what they were hearing.

"In most cases, if the parents are fit enough, they can donate, so we'll start there."

"Sign me up too!" Cocaine yelled. He would go first if necessary.

"And how long do you think I can survive on one kidney? Just from your professional opinion?" Lexxy asked.

"Several months, maybe a year. Your body has gone through a lot of trauma in such a small amount of time. Your one kidney would be doing the job for your entire body. Some people can live without both, but your case is special."

A year sounded like a lot of time, but it wasn't. Lucky was now regretting the time he'd spent away from Lexxy and hoped that she could get a kidney in time. He loved her, and he blamed himself partially because if he would've done what he was supposed to as a boyfriend, none of this would be happening.

"Well, thank you, Doctor. I need time to discuss my options with my family."

"Absolutely. I'm glad to see you up and alert. You have a lot of people here who love you."

The doctor nodded his head and walked out of the room, leaving Lexxy to figure out her next move.

CHAPTER 21

"Well, I just wanted to come and see you for myself to see how you were. I didn't really know what to expect, but now that I've laid eyes on you, I feel better."

Cocaine couldn't stop his eyes from mentally or physically rolling. He thought Lucky was soft. If he was a real nigga, who clearly wanted his chick back, he would've came in here ready to rumble, but he wasn't about that life, but Cocaine was. He was ready to check him and let him know it was time to leave, but Lexxy could sense Cocaine's anger, and she knew she needed to avert the situation herself so Cocaine didn't have to. She hadn't known him to be a dangerous person, not really, but now that she knew what he was capable of, she didn't want to leave it to chance, not like this.

"Lucky, thank you for coming to visit me. I appreciate it, but I think it's time for you to go."

Lucky was stunned by what she had to say; it was written all over his face. He couldn't believe she was asking him to leave when he came to check on her.

His mouth flew open, but he understood. He knew he wasn't wanted there, and above all, he knew it was fucking inappropriate for him to be there, and to have gone in before Denise even. He was doing too much, and Cocaine didn't want to upset Lexxy, but he was just seconds away from lettin' this nigga have it.

Lucky gave Lexxy pleading eyes, not wanting to leave, but with a raise of her eyebrow, she got her point across easily, and he knew it was time to go.

"I'ma check in with Denise in a few days and see how you doin', cool?"

"That—"

"Yeah homeboy, now get the fuck up outta here!" Cocaine interrupted Lexxy, throwing Lucky out the room.

Lucky knew Cocaine was about that life, and he didn't want to challenge him, furthermore, he knew Lexxy wanted him to go, so he went on about his business.

Lexxy looked up at Cocaine and smiled. She raised her arm to meet his cheek, and she caressed it softly. She now knew how Cocaine must have felt when she told him to leave months ago when she was in the hospital for the fire. She saw the look of defeat on Lucky's face, and even though she didn't see that or sense that from Cocaine, she could only imagine that it had to be a similar feeling.

Cocaine met her hand with a kiss, kissing the sides, and the inside of her palm. He felt terrible for what he'd done, and he knew now he'd have to face the music.

"Baby, I'm—"

"Shhh….I don't want to hear it, baby. I know you're sorry. I heard you while I was resting. I know you're sorry, but what I want to know is what happened? Tell me why in that moment you just shot off like that? I was standing right there, Cocaine."

Cocaine pulled his chair back up to the bed and sat down, and he looked Lexxy deep in her eyes, afraid of what she might say when he told her the truth.

"Honestly, a nigga wasn't even thinkin'. When I saw him, I mean really saw him, it was like I had a quick flash of my father's face, and I fuckin' lost it. It was reckless and dangerous, and I'm so, so sorry. I can never apologize enough, and now, you really in this mess because of me. Baby, I'll give you both kidneys if I have to."

Lexxy shook her head and took a deep breath. She didn't want Cocaine carrying this around. She loved him so much, and she hated seeing him this way. Most people would hate him, break up with him, probably try to kill him too, but she just couldn't do it. She couldn't see herself breaking up with the man she loved, especially when her father was to blame for the foolishness and stupid shit that had gone on.

"If you wanna get rid of a nigga, I feel that because I can't say if the shoe was on the other foot, I wouldn't be wantin' to let you go, but you gotta do what you think is best."

Lexxy laughed, and it was small at first, but then it grew, and grew, and soon, it filled the whole room. Cocaine assumed it was the drugs she was probably high on, but it wasn't.

"Nigga, you think you gon' shoot me and then get to

call the shots? That is the funniest thing I've heard all year. If anything, now you owe me. You owe me happiness, life, love, and a lifetime of it, so don't be tryna get rid of me so easily."

Cocaine had done more crying in this day than he'd ever done in his life. Hearing those words come out of Lexxy's mouth was like hearing angels sing for the first time. It was heavenly and fulfilling. He leaned over the bed and pressed his juicy lips against hers, filling the moment with love and lust, passion and fury. Their lips exploded with what could only be known in the movies as fireworks, and Lexxy wrapped her arms around her man, whispering how much she loved him in his ear, so if he ever doubted, he knew it now.

The crazy thing was, Lexxy should've been pissed. She should have been mad because she was shot over a fifteen-year-old beef, and she was mad, but not with Cocaine; but with her father. Her father was out of line, and there were skeletons in his closet that were clearly falling out. Lexxy just hoped this was going to be the only one to be making an appearance.

.***

Doctor Graham knew how all too often, a patient seemed optimistic, but on the inside, the shock of hearing something so serious could really mess them up. Lexxy had a very proactive family, and he could tell that by how much they were checking on her and asking if there was anything they could do. Though the doctor wanted to give Lexxy a chance to speak with her family first, there were so many things to consider in such a small amount of time, and she'd been taking longer than she should have with her guests, so the doctor felt it was only right for him to be honest and let her parents know, so there wouldn't be so much shock when Lexxy finally discussed it with them. Lexxy's body was weak, and she wasn't strong enough to really deal with the shock and confusion of their reactions if she was the first one to tell them.

The doctor came over to Junie and Wild Bill. Wild Bill was determined not to leave, even though Dutch was being a child and wouldn't stay.

"Well, Doctor?" Junie asked as Doctor Graham approached her.

The doctor placed his hands on his hips as he looked into Junie's eyes. He could tell she was hoping for the best and for good news, even if there wasn't any to give.

"Well, it seems as though she'll need a transplant once we remove the kidney that's causing her a lot of trouble."

"A transplant?" Junie gasped as she grabbed at her chest. If she didn't know any better, she would say she was having a heart attack; though she hoped that wasn't the case.

Wild Bill placed his arms around Junie's waist, trying to steady her. He just knew she was about to fall out.

"And how soon can we do that? Where will the transplant come from?" Junie asked, regaining her composure.

"Well, that depends. If any of her family is a good candidate and is willing to donate, it could be almost immediate. If not, then she'll go on a donor waiting list."

Junie couldn't fathom her child having to wait for anything, not her life and damn sure not a fucking kidney.

"We understand, Doctor. I need to speak to my husband and see how he wants to go about this."

"I agree, but just know, you all should be making moves as quickly as possible. Though Lexxy is stable now, her kidney could collapse and cause her further issues. It would be best to know what direction we're headed in in the event of something going poorly."

"I understand completely."

The doctor shook her hand and turned away.

Junie looked at Wild Bill with sickness in her eyes. She felt terrible, and her stomach hurt with anxiety. She had to keep it together for the ones around her, like Denise who couldn't control her throwing up. She was always a queasy one as a child, but this was like the exorcist. It just kept coming out. Junie wasn't ready to give the news to Denise because she knew she couldn't handle it. She knew she wouldn't be able to take it, so she kept it to herself for the moment, only discussing it with Wild Bill. Besides, she needed some time to get her words together, especially so she could talk to Dutch.

After Lucky came out of the room, Denise waited almost an hour before she went in. Junie was glad when she finally did make it though because she didn't know how much more of her throwing up everywhere she could take, and she knew that they were missing each other. She didn't want to see Lexxy until after everyone else did. Junie hoped that seeing everyone's smiling faces and happiness would warm her up, and when she went in, she would be happy and not looking sick like she imagined she would. Denise and Junie both were doing the best they could to keep their composure, but being strong for others was hard especially when breaking seemed so much easier.

After several hours of waiting to hear something, Dutch finally came back to the hospital. He knew it was childish of him to have left, but he was mad. He hated that Junie was taking a stranger's side over his. They were married, they were in love, yet, she felt the need to take Cocaine's side over his. Was he really that wrong? Of course he was, but he couldn't see that himself. He couldn't see what Junie was telling him, and he didn't care to. To him, it didn't matter the situation; Cocaine was in the wrong, and he wasn't. After all, it was an attempt on his life.

When he got back to the hospital, Wild Bill felt it would be best if he left. He couldn't go in there and see Lexxy like that, and with all the arguing going on around him, it was hard for him to concentrate and relax. Seeing Dutch reappear only made him angry because he couldn't seem to get it together, and he was almost embarrassed. Wild Bill was the crazy one, and he was never afraid, nor was he usually hesitant to pop off, but all he could think about was his niece and how he didn't want to further upset her, and he knew if he stayed, he'd be more than upset; he'd probably get violent.

Wild Bill said goodbye to Junie and Dutch, and he

left, hoping for the best and that they'd come up with a way to save Lexxy.

Junie sat down in her seat, waiting for Dutch to say something, anything, even though she knew she needed to tell him about the transplant. She didn't know how to break it to him. Hell, she didn't know how he would take it since he wasn't responding very well to anything else that day. He was acting bat shit crazy, and right now, they needed to be rational, not acting a fool.

"Dutch," Junie said reaching for his hand. Though she was mad, she had to go ahead and get it off of her chest. It felt like a weight on her heart that was making her sink deeper and deeper, and she hoped that by telling him, it would somehow relieve some of the pressure and stress they were feeling, and the faster they were able to accept what needed to be done, they could start making some shit happen.

Dutch looked over at Junie with questionable eyes. He didn't want to say anything because she clearly had something she needed to say.

"They're saying…they're saying that she needs a transplant, Dutch. Her kidney is failing her, and she needs to find a suitable donor as soon as possible."

Dutch immediately felt like he couldn't catch his breath. Like he couldn't breathe.

"Ok, so how do we find her a kidney? Should I contact Ralph? You know he knows about that black market stuff."

Junie couldn't believe he would even think about doing something illegal right now. That was not the way to go, and they didn't know where those kidneys came from. They could've been dirty or AIDS ridden. Junie wouldn't risk further hurting Lexxy, so they were going to do this the legal way and do whatever they could to make it so that they could save their daughter.

"No! Listen to you, you just don't know how to do anything the right way anymore, do you? That's crazy. We're going to all get tested and see if we're viable candidates, and if we are, or at least if I am, I will gladly sacrifice my kidney or my life for her."

Dutch couldn't agree more. He would do anything for his little girl. Even though he hadn't been in to see her yet and was acting like an idiot, there wasn't anything he wouldn't do for her. He loved her even more than he loved his own wife, his own life, and he would do what it took to ensure her health.

"Ok, so how do we begin testing?"

"I'll go talk to the doctor, you go in and see your daughter, and so help me God, if you're not on your best behavior, I will never forgive you. You can't keep acting out because you're mad and feeling guilty, because you have to remember, this is truly no one's fault but yours."

Junie kissed him atop his head as she walked over to the nurse's station to see how they could go about the testing.

Dutch did as Junie said and took himself into the room to see his daughter. When he walked in, Cocaine's head rested in her lap, and they were both asleep. Though he didn't want to wake her, he did want to speak with her, but now wasn't the time.

He tried tiptoeing back out of the room, but Cocaine woke up as he was leaving, and he followed after him.

They both needed to exchange a few words with one another. Cocaine was careful not to let the door slam as he walked out, and he met up with Dutch as he was about to take his seat.

"Dutch," Cocaine called out to him as he bent his knees to get comfortable in his seat.

The sound of Cocaine's voice made Dutch want to haul off and back hand his ass, but he promised he would be on his best behavior, so he figured he wouldn't get into it with him right now.

Cocaine took a seat next to him, and he spoke from his heart.

"Look, I don't fuck with you, and I wish you was dead, or at least on that bed and not her, but we both got the same goal; save my baby's life, so I'ma get tested and see if I can give her a kidney, and I'm sure you gon' do the same. This right here, this static between us, it ain't over, it's just put on hold. We gon' have our day, believe that, but today, and until Lexxy is better, we gotta deal with that. We both gotta live with the responsibility of seeing to it that she gets better."

Though Dutch hated Cocaine, he couldn't agree more. This definitely wasn't over, and he would have the final say so, and he would be the one to come out alive after all of this, whether Cocaine knew it or not. To Dutch, Cocaine was just a mad little boy, but what he didn't realize was, and he seemed to be underestimating Cocaine, was that when it came down to it, Cocaine would show him the real nigga that lived inside of him, the kind he was groomed to be from birth.

"I couldn't agree more," Dutch responded as Junie

came back over to their seats. Shortly after, Denise reemerged from the bathroom she couldn't stay out of. She'd seen Lexxy for a few minutes before she wound up passing out, and that was perfect for her because that was all she could take, and even though she knew she shouldn't, something told her to text Lucky. She had never liked him much when he and Lexxy were together, but to see him stepping up and being there for her like this, this was something she'd never seen before. She text him and let him know that Lexxy was resting and that she'd text with an update once she had one.

"So, the nurse said the doctor will be right with us."

The doctor took no time coming out and speaking with each of them who were there. Denise and Junie would have to undergo a different series of testing because they were women, and they needed to make sure everything about them was healthy, and rule out the risk of breast cancer, so they would both have to have mammograms, and even have tests done on their uterus and ovaries for ovarian cancer risks, but they were all willing to do it. The doctor let them know the week ahead would be a long one because it would take about that long for them to complete all the tests. Until then, Lexxy was to remain in the hospital so they could monitor her and make sure that she continued to be stable.

"So, are you all going to be tested?" the doctor asked, making sure he was on the same page.

"Yes," everyone said in unison. If nothing else, they were all in agreement about one thing—saving Lexxy's life.

CHAPTER 23

Three weeks later…

After all of the testing and the results coming back, none of them were a match. Not Dutch, Junie, Cocaine, nor Denise, and Wild Bill knew his kidneys had gone to shit long ago. He couldn't even pee without feeling his kidneys move around, so he knew he wasn't going to be a good candidate.

With no hope from any of them because their blood types, or they weren't in the best physical shape, or their kidneys just weren't right for them to be given to Lexxy.

Though time seemed to be running out, there were more options, and there were still a few tricks they could pull out of their hats if they were proactive and paid attention.

Doctor Graham hated giving them the bad news, and he hated giving Lexxy the bad news even more. She was trying to be strong for her family, because when she thought about herself, it just made it harder. She didn't know if she was going to make it out of this alive. She hoped she would, but she more so hoped that her family would be able to heal properly in the event things went south. She hoped they didn't, and she was being as positive as she could be, but she was also being realistic because she knew the chances of her getting a kidney in time were slim to none.

Her placement on the list was at the very bottom. There were one hundred people on the list who needed this sort of kidney. It was a very rare blood type, and Lexxy was still fairly young, so she needed a kidney that was still young, but full grown, and that would be of use to her for long term so she would never have to undergo another transplant, which was common for most people to have two, sometimes three because there was no way of telling if the kidney was one hundred percent perfect or functional long term; it just wasn't.

Because Lexxy had such a rare kidney type, she wasn't able to go on more than one donor list. She had to stay on one, and the list wasn't local either. In the event she did find a donor, it would have to be flown in, and they could only hope it would happen in enough time.

Even with all the money in the world, it was almost impossible for the family to get Lexxy's name moved up on the list. It was hard bribing people and finding people who were in charge of the lists, and the people who made them to somehow move her up. Cocaine thought of the idea first; he was the one who had mentioned it. With Ralph's help, Dutch's black market guy, they were able to find someone who worked heavily on one of the lists, and they were preparing to pay him off to get her name moved up. Even with the money they were willing to pay, they could only bribe her so far up the list without it alerting someone to what they were doing.

Cocaine had the money ready to meet the man, but

when he was supposed to meet up with him, the guy never showed.

He tried to reach him for days, several at a time, and no one ever responded. He felt like he failed his one true love, like he couldn't provide for her and be the man she needed him to be, and that wasn't even the case. It wasn't him who was inadequate. He'd done everything he was supposed to do, but sometimes, there were people who were willing to go just a little bit further than others. Cocaine didn't want to get anyone in trouble, and he didn't want the authorities to catch on to what they were doing, so he was trying to be slick about it, but that of course didn't stop Dutch from going further and pushing the envelope even more.

"Listen, John, is it? I know what you've been offered, but I'm willing to offer you more if you're willing to do the job."

"Oh, I don't know, Mr. Dutch, the authorities watch these lists heavily, and they pay close attention to the rate in which the donor list moves, you don't want that type of heat on you."

"You don't get to tell me what I want. What I want is for my daughter to be able to live her life. I won't let her die if there's anything I can do about it. I have the money; you just need to be willing."

Dutch had beat Cocaine out, and he did it on purpose. Dutch hated that Cocaine was trying to one up him, or at least that's how he felt, but that wasn't the case. Cocaine wasn't trying to beat anyone; he was trying to be a good man and help fix the problem he created, no matter what it took, within means. He didn't want to get John in trouble, and he didn't want a federal problem on his hands. He couldn't be marked by the Feds—that just wasn't going to end right period.

With the money invested, and Lexxy's name in the top fifty, she now had a better chance of living and finding someone to donate the kidney, whether living or dead.

Though Lexxy was doing her best to stay positive, she couldn't deny the pain she felt in her body, or the pain that ached in her heart. Every time she used the bathroom, it hurt to even hold her body over the toilet, and she wanted to go home. She just wanted to be in her own bed.

There weren't enough books in the world to keep her mind occupied, and no matter how hard she tried, she couldn't bring herself to accept the fact that she would probably die and leave Cocaine. Until she'd met him, her life had been routine, boring even. Sure, she had a drug lord for a father, but her personal life was simple. She was a student, a friend, and Lucky's girlfriend, very basic, and now, she was not only a drug lord's daughter, but she was a doctor, had a vengeful, hood love in her man Cocaine, and she was more alive than she'd ever been, or at least she had been, until now.

Every day, she felt closer to the brink of death, and she just hoped that her time wouldn't expire before she got to do some of the things she wanted to do, like get married, have children, if she even could at this point. She wanted to continue saving lives, delivering babies, and continue to grow as a woman, but she didn't know if that was going to be possible.

Days went by before Cocaine found out about what

Dutch had done, thanks to Junie who didn't believe in keeping secrets between family, and he didn't want to mention it to Lexxy because he wasn't no snitch, and besides that, he had something for Dutch…he was just waiting his time out. He'd waited fifteen years, what was a few more months?

The longer Lexxy lie in bed, the more time she had to think, which whether her father realized it or not, wasn't working out in his favor.

Lexxy rolled away from the door, shielding the tears she'd been desperately trying to keep in. Everything that was happening to her just didn't seem fair, but even then, she wasn't mad at Cocaine. How could she be? She loved him, and beyond that, she realized her father was being ignorant. She needed answers, and she needed them now.

She pressed the help button on the side of her bed, though it was for medical use or specifically for the nurse to help her, she needed a different kind of help. She needed to speak with her father immediately. She'd been avoiding this conversation for too long, but now, it was time for them to have it.

The nurse came on over the intercom speaker, "Yes?" the woman on the other end said pleasantly.

"Yes, is my father outside? If so, I need to speak with him please."

The woman on the other end giggled. She thought it was sweet that she wanted to speak with her father, but what she didn't know was Lexxy was about to let it rip on his ass.

Immediately after ending the intercom communication, Dutch walked in with his hands in his pocket and his head held down. He loved Lexxy with all of his heart, and her not wanting to see him killed her, and even though he was happy she finally wanted to see him, he knew it couldn't be good. She was finally awake and ready to face the demon that lived in him long ago, and occasionally awoke every now and then.

Lexxy tried propping herself up some so she could look him in the eye, but she was struggling. She was still very weak from all the surgery she had undergone.

Dutch, noticing she was in pain and could use a hand, walked over to her, hurriedly, and fluffed her pillows for her to lay back on.

She side eyed him the whole time. Even him being near her made her sick. She envisioned herself vomiting the closer he got to her, but she had to keep it together.

"Have a seat," she said to him as she motioned her arms toward the chair.

Dutch went over to the nearby table and grabbed a seat, pulling it closer to her.

"Yeah, you keep on holding your head down because you feel shame, and you should! You better tell me something, Daddy. Something that will turn this thing around because as of right now, I'm so mad at you, I could kill you myself!"

"I wish you would. I wish you'd take my suffering away. Seeing you in this bed is killing me. Knowing I can't help you in anyway is a father's worst nightmare."

"Stop worrying about me and worry about Cocaine! He was in the warehouse, Daddy, he saw you kill his father. Why? Was it retaliation for something he did to you? What was it?"

Dutch thought about his words carefully before he spoke. He didn't want to lie, nor did he want to say the wrong thing, but he knew whatever he said, it was going to be bad, so he just had to let the words flow.

"You see, baby, shit in the game is not easy. It don't always go the way you think it will; it just don't. At first, I wasn't gon' kill Juaqeen. I had it in my mind to just rob him, but shit got fucked up, and I got cocky, baby. I followed him and watched him. He ain't have a Wild Bill on his team. He had some good hittas, but they weren't strong enough. We were in the middle of a street war, and everybody had to be out to get theirs, and I was. I wanted you and your mama to have the finer things, so I did what I had to do. I snuck into that warehouse with the intentions of just robbing him, but the longer I sat there, the angrier I got, and the more I wanted what he had, baby, and I got it."

Tears poured from Lexxy's eyes as she thought about Cocaine as a small boy having to see his father's murder, and then the murderer go free with no type of justice. She couldn't believe her father did some shit out of envy. She'd never seen that side of him, but how could she? What was it to be envious of when you'd taken out the competition and taken what was his...what was his? That question rang loudly in her head. She wondered what it was that he took from Cocaine's father that he felt he was entitled to.

"What did you take, Daddy? Is it something you can give back?"

An evil smile crept across Dutch's lips. He could give it back, but why would he?

"I took his legacy, the only thing that he loved more than his own son..."

"What was it? Stop playing games with me! If you can give it back, just give it back!"

"Why would I? I'm not giving him back shit. That belongs to me, and everything else I got that day, it's mine! You may not be well versed in the street life, but I am. The worst thing you can do to a man is take away his mean to provide, his legacy. His life didn't mean shit without it, and if I give it back, and the rest, Juaqeen will just have been a martyr. I'm not doin' that."

"But what is it? Just tell me what it is!"

Dutch leaned over and whispered in her ear what it was, and her heart nearly broke into a million pieces.

"Daddy, if you don't give it back, I'll never forgive you, never. I'll hate you as long as there is breath in this weak ass body of mine."

After hearing that news, Lexxy's breathing sped up, her heart palpitating at a faster rate. She couldn't take this, and she didn't know if Cocaine knew or not. If she kept this secret, it could ruin their relationship, and if she did tell him, her father would be dead for sure...

After weeks of not being at the hospital, Wild Bill finally broke down and came back to see Lexxy, and this time, he vowed that he wouldn't leave her side. Her door was open, and he went in to see her watching TV. She never really watched it before, but being at the hospital so much turned her into a binge watcher.

"Hey, baby girl," Wild Bill said as he approached her bed. Her eyes lit up. She had been in contact with her uncle through text, but she hadn't seen him in weeks, and her heart was beginning to break at the thought that he didn't want to be around her.

"Hey, Unc! I'm so happy to see you! I missed you so much!" Lexxy reached her arms up like a little girl, waiting for her uncle to wrap his arms around her like he did when she was a little girl.

Seeing all the tubes and lines hooked into her body made Wild Bill nervous. He didn't want to hurt her or accidentally pull something out, so him reaching out to her frightened him, but the more her face went from happy to sad, it changed his heart, and melted it. He couldn't deny her.

He leaned over and grabbed her into his strong arms,

and though he didn't want to, he cried like a newborn baby who needed milk. He was hurting for Lexxy. He was hurting for his family, and he didn't want this for her. He wished he could do something to make her feel better, but for now, he had to settle for just being there physically and trying to compose himself to be there for her emotionally.

"Oh, Unc, not you too. I expect this from them," she said, pointing her head toward the door to where her family had been in and out of.

"I'm sorry baby, so tell me what's new?" Wild Bill took a seat next to her and listened attentively.

"Well, you know about the failed donor situation, right? They haven't found anyone yet—"

"No, I mean in your personal life. You and Cocaine ok? I heard about the fight you had with your father."

Lexxy took a deep breath, not wanting to go back to that moment even in her mind, especially since she was harboring a secret that could potentially ruin her relationship with her man, but she had to tell Wild Bill something, and in a way, he was like her friend. He always listened to her and gave advice as he saw fit or whenever he wanted to really, but today, he just wanted to listen.

"Cocaine and I are fine I suppose. I told him I forgive him...after all, this shit wasn't his fault; it was Daddy's, so I couldn't be mad at him even if I wanted to, ya know?"

Wild Bill nodded his head. He knew exactly what she meant. He too was mad at his best friend for what he had done because of the problem it caused, but it went even deeper than that. Wild Bill hoped he never had to reveal just how deep it truly went.

As Lexxy continued talking, Wild Bill thought back to the day Lexxy was born, and how everything played out without him.

"Wild Bill, you got mail!" the CO said as he approached Wild Bill's cell. At this point, Wild Bill had been in prison for six months, and he had five years left to go on his sentence. He got caught up on a murder charge, and instead of doing twenty years in prison, he was able to do five and parole out but still belong to the state for the next ten years. He'd fucked around and killed the wrong person, and now he was having to do the time. But, he did it for Dutch. Everything he did was always for him, for Junie, for the family dynamic they'd created.

Wild Bill reached his hand out to grab the mail, and it was several envelopes bundled into one. Wild Bill had no family, no woman, no nothing, so he didn't know who would be sending him mail because he and Dutch talked frequently. Granted, it was always business for the most part and occasionally pleasantries, but that was hardly ever.

Wild Bill tore into the first letter, and at the top written in large letters, it said Junie's name. Of course, she cared more for Wild Bill than Dutch; she'd always been a real friend to him.

His eyes skimmed the letter to make sure nothing was wrong, and as he read the letter, he realized there was nothing wrong; in fact it was the exact opposite.

"Bill, we waited to tell you for just in case, but we're having a baby, a sweet baby girl. We were afraid to tell you in case we were being watched. With everything that's been going on, it's barely safe to send mail, but hopefully this finds you

peacefully and safely. Hopefully, when this letter gets to you, our secret will still be safe about the baby. Dutch and I discussed it, and we want you to be her God father. Her name will be Alexxis, Lexxy for short. You're more than just an uncle or a God father, you're family. We love you, stay strong, stay up."

Wild Bill couldn't believe it! He was going to be an uncle, well, a God father. That would be the greatest achievement of his life.

He wondered when they found out they were pregnant. He didn't mind the secret part though, he knew how it was in the street life, and he didn't want any of them to be hurt or their lives be threatened.

He went on to open the next letter, and as he pulled out the paper, several pictures fell out of it, hitting the floor. He picked up the pictures, and they held precious memories of Dutch, Junie, and Lexxy. She was the cutest baby he'd ever seen in his life.

Wild Bill opened the paper and began reading the next letter.

"When I wrote the previous letter, I saved it to mail out with this one for just in case, but your beautiful God daughter has been born, and she is amazing and very aware. She's got that beautiful chocolate skin like Dutch. Bill, you're always in our thoughts and prayers. Call home, I'd love to hear from you, and don't worry, I promise to keep you updated on the baby. You won't miss a thing. When you come home, she'll know all about her God father-uncle, what a weird title, but she'll know exactly who you are, and I know you'll protect her with your life. We love you..."

That letter Junie sent him was something he still had to this day. Lexxy was his saving grace. When he first went to prison, he planned to stir up trouble so he could go straight to seg and be left the fuck alone, but after seeing Lexxy and knowing that he was being missed, he wanted to do everything he could to stay out of trouble so he could go home when it was time with no delays.

Those moments would forever be etched into his brain, and as he talked to Lexxy, he realized how much pain he would always be in for missing her birth.

"Unc, you listening? Unc?" Lexxy asked.

"Yeah baby, I'm sorry, keep talkin. My mind went somewhere else for a second."

"I see. You ok?"

"Yeah, I'm good. Go ahead."

Lexxy kept talking, and Wild Bill did his best to listen, that is until Dutch walked in barking orders.

"Damn Bill, I've been looking for you. I need you to go handle some business for me."

"Nah, I can't do that. I'm chillin' with niecey-Pooh right now."

"Nigga, that wasn't a request. Get yo ass up. You got shit to do."

Wild Bill turned his head to the side, confused as to who he was talking to, and he went back to talking to Lexxy.

"Bill, now, Nigga!"

"Daddy, what is the rush? He just got here."

"Mind your business, Lexxy. I don't pay this nigga to babysit. Get yo ass up before you get thrown off the payroll."

Since Lexxy had been in the hospital, Wild Bill had been getting told what to do in the worst way, and he knew it was because Dutch was upset, but he wasn't going to take too much more disrespect from his ass.

"It's cool, baby girl. I'ma go ahead and go. I love you, and I'll be back later."

Wild Bill kissed Lexxy and headed out of the room. If looks could kill, Dutch would've had a hollowtip in his forehead. This nigga was really tripping.

With all of the time they'd spent in the hospital, together, Junie still felt like she didn't know Cocaine, and like she could share a little bit of wisdom with him. She wanted him to know that regardless of the mistake, they were family, and it was all of their faults for not having settled certain things. Junie never had a hatchet to bury, but she wanted to know if it was possible for Cocaine to bury his with her husband.

She saw the way he looked at Lexxy, and she knew from experience that love could be a rocky road, especially when murder was involved, and she didn't want her love taken away, but even more so, she didn't want the revenge that Wild Bill would for sure have to carry out against him if he did kill Dutch ruin what Lexxy and Cocaine had.

In her mind, she hoped with her motherly love and kind words, she could fix this situation. She'd invited Cocaine out to lunch with her, and he actually liked her. He thought she was a wonderful mother, and a good ally to have on your team in the event some shit went wrong. She was calm and very understanding, something he wasn't used to from anyone except Lexxy, so he knew where she got it from.

He was at the hospital checking on Lexxy when he received a text on his phone.

"Meet me for lunch today, downtown, my treat. We can go to Café Coco if you'd like, if you haven't been."

Initially, Cocaine thought Lexxy might have had something to do with it, so he mentioned it to her to see what she would say.

"Oh, so you think you slick, havin' your mama meet me for lunch. Y'all plottin' against me. I knew it." He laughed.

Lexxy's eyebrows furrowed in confusion. She had no idea what the hell he was talking about.

"Cocaine, what are you talking about now?" Lexxy asked as she sat up on her pillows and turned the TV down so she could hear him better.

"Your mama just invited me to lunch. She said it was her treat, but you know I ain't finna let no woman, especially my future mother-in-law pay for no meal for me, but I'ma let her think that 'til I pick up the tab."

"I honestly don't know what you're talking about, babe. I haven't even talked to mom today, so…she came up with that plan all on her own."

Cocaine thought about it, and it was true. He'd been with Lexxy that entire morning, so surely she wasn't able to slip nothin' like that past him.

"I wonder what she wants…oh God, hopefully it isn't more bad news, or strange news. Maybe it won't be news at all."

"Then what could she want?"

Lexxy shrugged her shoulders. She didn't know what

her mother wanted. She hadn't run the idea past her first, so it could have been a number of things. She just hoped whatever it was, it wasn't something that would further piss either of them off. She was already on iffy terms with her father; she didn't want to be on the same terms with her mother or her boyfriend, so she decided it would be best if she just waited it out to see what was going on.

"Did she give you a time?" Lexxy asked.

He then looked at his phone and received another text message that said at eleven. That wasn't really lunch, but that was ok. He was going to go and see what she wanted. He worried just a little bit though. He didn't have that much mom training, so he hoped she wouldn't be asking him any crazy questions or anything that would be too hard for him to answer because Cocaine wasn't big on lying, and he wasn't going to period. Regardless of the situation, he was an honest dude.

"Yeah, she said eleven, but I ain't really dressed for lunch, baby."

Cocaine looked down at himself and saw his gray sweatpants, and Lexxy noticed them as well.

"You damn right you ain't dressed for lunch. Why don't you go home and change your clothes before I have to leave this hospital and show the fuck out."

"Mmm…my feisty baby. Don't you worry, I ain't dickin' nobody down but you, and I can't even get that right now, so I'm good. You the only one I want any way, my queen."

Cocaine slowly but gently climbed into bed with Lexxy and started kissing on her. He didn't give a damn that she wasn't well; he loved her, and she was still the most beautiful woman in the world to him. She had good days, and bad days, but today was a good one, and he was gon' milk it as long as he could. Lexxy knew they shouldn't be getting fresh in the hospital, but she couldn't help it. She needed this attention from Cocaine, and she wanted it. Just because her kidney was fucked up, her pussy wasn't, nor were her hormones. Every time she saw Cocaine, her pussy still got wet, and she still wanted him inside of her all the time. It was hard for her to be around all that man and not want him.

"Stop, boy, you gotta go home and change."

"Mh-mm…I'ma go in a minute," Cocaine said as he kept kissing her down her neck. He reached underneath her hospital gown and felt the moistness between her legs.

"Damn, baby, you want this, don't you?" he whispered as he blew into her ear.

"Ye-yess…" she trembled with delight.

Cocaine didn't give a fuck if someone walked in on him. He was going to please his woman at all costs. However she wanted it, he was going to give it to her.

His fingers were wet from love juice leaking down on him, so it was no problem for him to slide his fingers inside of her pussy and give her a little bit of pleasure. His dick was rock hard, and even though he couldn't stick his glorious dick inside of her tight hole, she still loved jacking him off.

Lexxy wiggled her fingers down to his dick, and she pulled it out of his sweatpants, letting it plop over the top and onto the crease of his pants.

Lexxy licked her fingers and started massaging his dick as he kept kissing on her and fingering her. Using his thumb, he played with her clit in between thrusts. Their bodies moved with one another, causing friction and fire in the best way between them.

"Shit, Cocaine. Uh!" Lexxy moaned.

"Shh….be quiet, baby. You know you don't want them people comin' in here, and I don't give a damn if they do, I'm not gon' stop fuckin' you just to save face."

Those words sent chills down Lexxy's spine. She loved the way he talked to her when they were being intimate with one another. It always drove her crazy.

Cocaine was bringing her to a climax, and besides the fact that her pussy had grown even warmer than it was before, her heart monitor was going off like crazy. He couldn't lie—it was something about it going off like that that he loved. He enjoyed knowing he was sending her into a sexual frenzy.

Her legs began tightening around his hand, but he didn't give a fuck, that just meant that he was doing his job. As her pussy grew wetter, his dick got harder, and he knew he was about to bust and spill all over her hand.

"Damn, Lexxy, I love you," he grunted as his cum was about to shoot out of the top of his giant dick.

"Cum for me, daddy," she said playfully, and she didn't have to say it again, or at all really because he was well on his way there.

As their orgasms reached new heights, they both let their love pour from one another, and onto each other's hands.

"Mmm…damn, baby, you the only person I ever let really jack me off. That shit be feelin' so good."

"Cocaine, stop talkin' like that, always bein' fresh."

"You like it, lil' baby."

Cocaine put his fingers in his mouth tasting Lexxy's pussy juice on his tongue, and even in the hospital, she still tasted good. Lexxy was still turned on and loved watching Cocaine taste her, and she missed tasting him too. She loved how sweet his nectar was, so she had to take a page from his book and swallow the kids he'd spilled onto her hand.

"Girl, you better watch yourself. That's how you get fucked."

Lexxy giggled, and she kissed the side of his cheek before he left.

Now, her mind was clear and free of whatever her mother and Cocaine were going to be talking about or doing. She busted her nut, and everything was all good.

After Cocaine went and changed his clothes, and felt that he was suitably dressed, he took off to meet Junie at Café Coco. He'd never been, but when he looked online at their menu, something he found himself doing more often since he got with Lexxy, the menu seemed to be good and like it could accommodate him, so he had no issues with that.

He got to the restaurant and text Junie to let her know he'd be right in once he parked his car. He parked and went straight inside. Immediately to his left, he spotted her out of the corner of his eye in a long, flowy, yellow dress covered with an all-white cardigan. To a normal person, Junie didn't look like the wife of a major drug or crime lord. She looked like she fit in with the women on Broadway with a corporate job. She had a fancy house already, but she was missing the good husband.

Junie rose from her seat and held her arms open for Cocaine.

"Hey, Cocaine, thanks for meeting me."

"Of course. How are you?"

When Cocaine smiled, she saw exactly what Lexxy saw; a very handsome, promising young man.

"I'm well, thank you. Have a seat, you hungry?"

"Starvin' to be honest. I looked online, and I already know what I'ma get. Who's our waiter?"

Junie called over the waiter and let Cocaine order before she started speaking. When he placed his order and what he wanted to drink, and the waiter walked off, Junie spoke.

"So, I know you're wondering why I asked you to lunch, so I'll get straight to it. I want to know if you'll bury the hatchet with my husband. Before you say anything, think about it like this; you and Lexxy, I don't see that going anywhere any time soon, at all, and you're a part of this family, and we can't have family trying to kill one another, you know what I mean?"

The waiter came by and dropped off his drink, and as he left, Cocaine took a sip of his drink, and then he answered Junie.

"As good as that sounds because I do love your daughter, I don't know if that's something I can do. I love her, and I don't want her to be unhappy, but what about me? My father would expect me to avenge him."

"Would he? Your father was big on family, and he would want you to be loyal to what you have now, not hold on to the past."

Cocaine looked at Junie surprised and a little upset about what she was saying.

"In all due respect, you don't know what my father would want. You didn't know him."

"I had a feeling you would say that. Let me show you something."

Junie reached into her purse and pulled out a manila folder.

"Here, take a look at these."

Cocaine ripped open the envelope and looked inside, and he couldn't believe his eyes.

"These have to be photoshopped!"

Cocaine continued going through the photos, and his eyes had to be deceiving him.

"No, they're real. I knew your father, well, we knew your father. We were all very close at one point in time. Dutch was one of his first soldiers initiated into the community."

Cocaine always figured he was in the gang; obviously, he wore the gorilla tattoo on his face, and that was all his father, but he never thought he was that high up, or that close with his father.

"I don't understand....please help me understand,"

Cocaine said as he covered his face with his hands. This was too much too fast. What could this mean?

"See, Dutch, back in the day, was crazy. His murder game was one of the coldest in the industry, and your father, Juaqeen saw something in him. He wanted him down on the crew to help take out the competition. Your father treated Dutch like a brother, like a friend, but one day, Dutch got tired of being on the bottom of the totem pole. He wanted more, as he always has. He wanted to be beside Juaqeen instead of behind him, and Juaqeen promised that eventually, he would promote him, but it never happened…I didn't know until the day you shot Lexxy that Dutch was the one who did this. It was always a mystery, and one that we all took hard, and that's why I feel so apologetic. I knew your father, and he was a good man, but he never looked to his past. He was always thinking of the future, and that's why I don't want you to be caught up on what was. You have to live for today."

The waiter brought their food to the table, and they sat there, staring at one another. Cocaine was trying his best to process all of this information, but he didn't know how, and he didn't know what she wanted him to say.

The lunch was over, and he'd had more than enough revelation for the day, really for a lifetime. To even think Dutch would betray his father in that way let him know he was more than just an opportunist; he was a real snake ass nigga, and that meant he really had to be dealt with. It was no way he could let that shit go now. Not after finding out the real truth behind what happened, and there were still so many questions he had, but he couldn't handle asking them today, not like this.

Instead, he went to the only place he ever found solace and happiness. He went back to Lexxy so he could finish filling her in on what took place. He'd already text her some of the details, but the rest would have to be discussed in person. He didn't even have the energy to keep texting about it.

Lexxy was sitting up smiling, waiting for him to come in, and when he did, he went straight to her and climbed in the bed with her.

"Tell me what happened, daddy."

Lexxy rubbed his head and listened to him spill how he felt and complain about her father. She felt his pain, and it only added more to how she was feeling before. She loved him and didn't want her man feeling this way, but what could she do? How could she make him feel better while pretending to feel ok herself? She couldn't.

As they lie there, Lexxy wished there was something she could do to help, but there was nothing she could do. Her father was her father, and she couldn't make him do anything. Even if he did apologize, there was no apology great enough to fix what he had done.

"Knock, knock!" the doctor said as he came in. Cocaine looked up, and they locked eyes.

"Hey, Doc, what's up?" Cocaine asked as he sat up and put his arm around Lexxy.

"'Well, I came down here to deliver some news."

"Good news, I hope," Lexxy admitted.

"May I sit down?"

Lexxy knew anytime someone wanted to sit down, it probably wasn't good.

"Of course, go ahead."

Doctor Graham pulled a chair over closer to the bed, and his face went from happy to very sad.

"Well, unfortunately, it looks like even with your name moving up on the list, which I'm not even sure how that was possible, but I'm not sure if you'll have enough time to wait it out. After running more tests, we have to remove that kidney immediately, and you won't last long on the one kidney. Lexxy, we're staying optimistic, but I wanted to at least let you know and tell you the truth because I know that's what you prefer; the straightforward nitty gritty."

Doctor Graham pulled his glasses back on his face and rose to his feet.

"Thank you, Doctor. Thank you for being honest."

Doctor Graham nodded his head and exited the room.

Cocaine was already holding Lexxy, but he held her even tighter. He could have squeezed his life out of him and into her.

He looked down at her, and she was crying. He felt it before he saw it. Her heart was breaking, and so was his.

"What do you want me to do, baby? Tell me what to do, and I'll do it, baby. Whatever you want me to do."

Lexxy gave a small smile and wished it was that easy.

She wished she could tell him what to do and he just do it, but there was nothing to be done. Lexxy was dying, and no one could fix her but God himself. Where was he when she really needed him now?

With more bad news about Lexxy, Cocaine wanted to do whatever it would take to make her happy and keep her alive. The thing was, her being in that hospital wasn't doing anything but frustrating her and the rest of the family, and it was bringing down everyone's moral, especially Lexxy. She hadn't been happy in so long, and now, with the possibility of her dying soon, her world was spinning out of control in a way that she never saw for herself.

Everyone dies; this was something that she knew. It was inevitable, and it would come for us all, but that didn't make it any easier or any better, especially when you were sick.

Lexxy had the surgery she needed to have her kidney removed, and that was a month ago. She was finally healed, and even though the doctors wanted to keep her to keep a special eye on her, she was ready to go home. Cocaine wasn't comfortable with her going home, so he had his house set up for home care.

He'd been trying to prepare Lexxy for the move ever since she got back situated from her surgery, but every time he brought it up, she would either have nothing to say or very little on the subject, and he was tired of bringing it up. It didn't matter if she didn't want to, she was going to be moving in with him, and that was going to be that on that.

She had finally been released from the hospital, against their wishes, but she was also tired of being there, and she knew whatever care she was going to get at home would at least be more comfortable than at the hospital. Though she had grown to really like the staff and she was used to them, she hated being laid up in the same place where all she saw was white or beige walls, and no cable. She'd grown to appreciate her cable channels now, and she wanted to get home to them so she could do some more binge watching, since that was all she was going to be able to do.

Going places would be difficult for her, especially since she was instructed to be on bed rest, but that wasn't her. If she was going home, she was going home, and she was going to enjoy herself. She didn't want to let herself die and be miserable. She didn't want to be unhappy and let her life be ruined. Lexxy took this as a sign that it was time to live like it was her last, since it was, but of course, all that shit was easier said than done.

"You ready to go, Sexy Lexxy?" Cocaine asked as he helped her into a wheelchair and wheeled her outside. He had his beautiful Rolls Royce, all-white of course, pulled up on the curb. He remembered Lexxy saying it was her favorite, and today, and every day for the rest of her life was all about her, period.

"As ready as I'll ever be, I guess."

When they got to the curb, Cocaine helped her into the car, and then he put her wheelchair into the trunk.

He thought she'd smile or at least be happy to see the car. She'd only ridden in it twice, but she wasn't. Her facial expression didn't even change. He knew she was depressed about her current condition, but there was something else going on that he needed to know about. He knew she was feeling miserable, but what could this be? She had her family's support, Denise, and him. All he needed was the love from his woman, and he hoped that that would be enough for her, but who was he kidding? She was dying, and no one knew how much time she had left on her life.

Cocaine had planned a surprise party for her when she got to the house, as a welcome home, housewarming kind of thing for her, but he could now see she wasn't in the mood, but it was too late. Everyone was already at his house, getting live in the five. The music was probably already going, everyone was probably already drinking.

Cocaine just hoped that Dutch didn't think he was invited, because he damn sure wasn't welcome in his home.

As they drove down the highway, Lexxy's eyes were glazed over, and she was in a different world. She was non-responsive, and no matter how Cocaine tried to reach her, she wouldn't answer him. Though he was frustrated, he didn't know what else to say, and he didn't know how to make her feel better, but there was nothing he could do at this point. They were almost home, and the party was all for her, so he just hoped that seeing her family and work friends would help perk her up.

"Well, we're home," Cocaine announced as he got out of the car and got her wheelchair out.

She looked out the window and up at the house. Even though she knew where she was going, she desperately hoped somehow, they'd pull up at her house, and that just didn't happen. She was looking at Cocaine's enormous house, the house that she once thought was beautiful now seemed like a prison to her. She felt like this was where she was going to die quietly and lonely. Even though Cocaine was so close, she was pushing herself away from him. She was mentally preparing herself to possibly die.

Cocaine came around the side and opened the door for her and he helped her into her seat, the seat of death as she was beginning to call it in her mind.

Cocaine made sure everyone parked in the back so Lexxy wouldn't see the cars and automatically know what was about to go down. He even had a ramp installed in the front of his house so it would be easier for Lexxy to get around on her own if she wanted to come outside, even though she wasn't supposed to. He didn't expect her to actually lie in bed the entire time; that would make anyone fucking crazy.

He wheeled her up the ramp and opened the door, and Denise noticed the door opening first and yelled, "Surprise!" and the others followed suit. Little blasts of the word surprise popped up and out of the mouths of everyone around her, and she felt extremely overwhelmed to the point where she broke down crying.

At first, Cocaine thought it was happy tears, that she was crying because she was happy, but when he came around, he saw the face she was making, and she was miserable. These were not tears of joy, they were tears of sadness.

Denise noticed right away what was happening, and she told everyone to stand back, and to move away from the door so Lexxy could get in and go be by herself.

Cocaine had moved everything downstairs to the guest bedroom so Lexxy would be more comfortable, and there was a big sign above the doorway with red streamers around it that said, "The Royal Quarters Await You."

As sweet as the gestures were, she wasn't feeling it, and she didn't want to be bothered with all of this. How was she supposed to be happy and be smiling in people's faces when she felt miserable on the inside?

She went into the bedroom and tried to slam the door behind her, but she didn't even have enough energy to do that after wheeling herself into the room.

Cocaine ran after her and found her in the middle of the room, crying her eyes out.

"Baby, what was all that about? What's the matter?"

He got down on the balls of his feet so he could be on the same level as she was. He hated the way he towered over her in that chair. He liked being as close to her as possible, and that chair was making that hard for them.

Lexxy wiped the tears away from her face as she thought about Lucky. This was the same exact scenario they'd gone through before. She was leaving the hospital and moved in with Lucky, and after only a short time of happiness, it was all over, and Lucky was gone. What was she going to find out about Cocaine? Did he have some type of family? What was she going to do?

"I just…baby, I don't know. I'm afraid. What if this is the end of our relationship? I moved in with Lucky and he snuck around with a secret family. I just can't have that happen again! I can't do it. I love you, Cocaine, but all of this might be too much, you taking me in, taking care of me, paying to have me have home care. Cocaine, I don't know. You don't owe me anything, and I don't want you to feel like you do."

That stung Cocaine's heart. Of course he owed her, but not for the reasons she probably thought. He owed her his life and his heart, and his loyalty, and that's what he was going to give her whether she wanted it or not.

Cocaine put her wheelchair in the stop position, and picked her up.

"Cocaine! Put me down!" she yelled.

He brought her over around to the side of the bed and slowly put her down, and then he crawled in on the other side.

"You right, I don't owe you shit, at least not for what you think. I love you, baby. I'm so fucking in love with you, and I wanna spend whatever time we got left together, and I don't give a fuck about none of that other shit you sayin' about that fuck boy. That nigga ain't know how to love you like me. He ain't know how to appreciate you like me, baby. I told you before, and I guess I gotta tell you again, but I ain't never lettin' you go. So, if you're done with all that lil' pity partyin' you tryna have, can we at least go join the real party that I worked real hard to make happen for you?"

The truth was, Lexxy didn't want to, and she damn sure didn't want to have to be wheeled around all fucking night.

"Under one condition, Cocaine."

"Name it, it's yours."

"Please let me walk. I don't wanna be all in that chair. It's uncomfortable, and I'm not an invalid."

"I don't know, baby. The doctor said not to let you overdo it, and I'm pretty sure walkin' around a mansion would be over doing it."

"Ok, what if I walk for a little while, and wheel it for a little while? I can switch it up if need be."

Cocaine knew he wasn't going to win this, and he wanted her to enjoy the party, so he agreed to let her do it her way.

Cocaine hated the fact that Lucky had ruined her heart because now it would be almost impossible for her to trust him all the way, but he would do everything in his power to make her trust him because even if she didn't know it, he was going to be her last lover ever. He would make her his forever, no matter how long their forever truly was.

Wild Bill stood at the bar in the kitchen, drinking, trying not to overdo it. He didn't want to upset Lexxy whenever she did make it back out, but as hard as he had been working, he needed a little release.

When Lexxy did reappear, she had a smile on her face, and she was walking with the help of Cocaine. He had her hand, walking her around the living room, smiling and trying to appear as everything was ok, but Wild Bill knew it was some bullshit. He could see right through the smiles and the happy faces.

From the moment he walked in Cocaine's house, Dutch had been blowing his phone up like a bitch. He was acting like a baby mama checkin' up on her nigga, and Wild Bill was tired of answering that nigga.

He wanted him to run his errands like he was some type of do boy, and that wasn't his job. Wild Bill was way more important and worked way too hard to be getting treated like some lil' nigga off the street. Something was going on with Dutch, and Wild Bill didn't know what it was, but it was something going on, and he hoped he would find out soon what it was.

When Lexxy finally made her way around to Wild Bill, she saw the confusion on her face. Though she wasn't in the best mood, she knew something was going on with her uncle, and she wanted to know what it was.

"I'm good right here, baby. I'ma talk to my uncle for a minute."

"If you need me, baby, I'ma be over here, ok?"

"Ok."

Lexxy went over to Wild Bill and leaned against the counter. "What's up, Unc?"

He looked up from his phone and noticed Lexxy was talking to him. "Here, baby girl, let me help you." Wild Bill helped her over to the dining room table so they could sit down and talk.

"So, how does it feel to be home, baby girl?"

"I don't know yet. It's gonna take some getting used to I guess. When me and Lucky did this, well, you know how that turned out. I can't deal with that again."

"I get the sense you ain't gotta worry about that with this one. Don't quote me on that but I feel confident about it."

"You psychic now? What's going on with you, Unc? Your face has been in that phone this whole time."

Wild Bill didn't know if he wanted to say anything or not. He really didn't, but he felt like he should tell her because things were going to shit fast.

"You know, Dutch has been working me to death. And it's been some bullshit too. I can't keep on playin with your daddy. I ain't no corner boy, no run around, and he's been treating me like I am. I mean, I don't mean to sound like no bitch, but I ain't that type, baby girl. Your father has been my partner for so long, but I'm starting to see some shit I don't like."

Lexxy knew all too well how Wild Bill felt. She was feeling that same way. He'd been on some stupid shit for some time now, and she was glad to have somebody to talk to about it with.

"Tell me about it. I didn't realize Daddy was so treacherous. He took something very important from Cocaine's father. I told him to give him it back, but he said there was no way he was going to do that, and the only reason I didn't tell Cocaine was because he doesn't even know Dad has it."

"What is it?" What does he have?" Wild Bill queried.

Lexxy leaned over and whispered in his ear what it was, hoping no one heard her, especially Cocaine, and Wild Bill's eyes got big.

"You serious?"

"Very."

Wild Bill didn't know what to say, but this was some crazy shit. Wild Bill now knew that he couldn't trust Dutch, that their entire friendship haD been based on a lie, a bigger lie than it was built on...Wild Bill never thought he was going to have to, but now he was going to have to talk to Cocaine. He had a lot of explaining to do...

"You ok, Unc?" Lexxy asked as Wild Bill's face went from normal to crazy as fuck in a few seconds.

"Yeah, yeah, I'm ok, baby. Look, stay right here, I'll be right back."

Wild Bill knew he had to find Cocaine right now. He needed to talk to him ASAP about what he just found out. Before he found him, he felt like fire had caught in his chest. What type of shit was this? Wild Bill's mind went back to a time he thought was long forgotten, to some shit he thought he'd never think about again, but with the information Lexxy just shared with him, that was going to be impossible.

The phone rang back in Wild Bill's ear. He had been calling Dutch for several days now trying to see if he had gone ahead with the plan they'd put in place five years before, and so far, it seemed like the plan was working, but Dutch wasn't picking up the phone.

As always, Wild Bill expected the worst whenever he didn't answer. He always assumed some shit went south when he couldn't reach Dutch, and he knew how reckless he could be, which was cool with Wild Bill, but they'd been working on this for far too long to let anything ruin the plan they'd come up with.

Wild Bill called Dutch back to back for an hour straight, hoping he'd pick up, and finally after his twelfth time calling, he answered.

"Hello?"

"Damn Dutch, I been callin'. What you got goin' on?" Wild Bill yelled into the phone.

"I was tryna make some shit shake, but it didn't work. The shit didn't go as expected."

"What you mean?"

Wild Bill was trying to make sure he understood what he was saying before he just assumed some shit on accident.

"It just didn't go as planned."

"Ok, but did you get the bricks, man? Did you get the gold?"

The line was quiet for a moment, but Dutch was breathing heavily as if he were running.

"Nah man, I didn't even get it. I had to get out before some shit popped off. It was some other niggas there; I couldn't handle business."

Wild Bill was shocked. He thought for sure the tip he'd gotten was a good one. He met a dude while he was in prison that told him about the golden bricks that Juaqeen had. He told him about the empire he was building and how successful it had become. Wild Bill then passed that information onto Dutch, thinking they were in it together, that they were brothers, and that they were going to be making a name for themselves in the streets, but that was never the case, and that was never Dutch's agenda. He wanted the streets, the gold, and the money for himself.

They were supposed to split the gold, and that was supposed to set Wild Bill up for life.

Wild Bill knew Dutch must've gotten away with something because not too long after that, he had a major come up.

Dutch had befriended Juaqeen to get his money, his connect, his everything, and Dutch didn't give a damn what he had to do to get it. What he wanted, he got, at all costs, no matter the consequences. He never had any thoughts of sharing the benefits with Wild Bill. He figured he did most of the leg work. He wasn't giving Wild Bill no damn finder's fee, period.

To most, those golden bricks were money…he could cash 'em in and make something really happen with them, but to Juaqeen, they were sentimental, they held more value than anyone could ever know.

Every golden brick was something special. One was all the gold jewelry he'd ever had, and he had it melted into one brick. He had a golden brick for when Cocaine was born, one for when he found out his girlfriend was pregnant, and so forth.

Several of them were fake though. Inside of the fake ones, there were letters from his mother, parts of her diary that he'd spaced out and kept for Juaqeen to have one day when he was old enough to understand, and more importantly, there were blueprints inside of them. Blue prints that would one day change the way the hood was made up. It would change the drug game. Juaqeen hated pushing drugs to his people, but he knew they needed 'em, but he was ready to elevate, to take it to the next level. He was tryna see corporate America, wipe them out, and take over. That was his plan. He fucked up and told the wrong people his business, and he had people watching him, following him, like Dutch.

Dutch was a snake, one of the yellow bellies that nobody should ever be around. He used Juaqeen, and he eventually killed him.

Now, all these years later, Wild Bill was under the impression that someone else did this to Juaqeen, that he must've been had by the supposed other people who were there that day, that Dutch never left with any of the stuff, but now, he knew that was a lie.

It was like a ton of bricks fell on his head all at once. How could this have happened? Now, he felt like he owed Cocaine an apology. This entire time, he'd been sleeping with the enemy, and none of them had anything to show for it except Dutch.

Wild Bill finally found Cocaine, and he did something he thought he'd never do; he told the story he'd kept locked away in his mind, a story that he didn't even realize had more parts to it, but he had to tell Cocaine. He wanted him to have peace of mind so that he could rest and take care of Lexxy, but he wouldn't be able to if he didn't know the truth, if he didn't have some type of closure.

Wild Bill got Cocaine's attention and told him he needed to speak with him in private.

They stepped outside onto the veranda, and Wild Bill began spilling his guts, telling him everything he had to say from beginning to end, and when he was done, the fire that had been lit inside of Cocaine a long time ago that he'd temporarily dimmed was burning bright once more. He wanted Dutch's ass, and he wanted what his father had for him.

After Wild Bill explained what happened, Cocaine felt bad for him. He'd been cut out of a major deal, and Wild Bill had become a lap dog. He always was one; but there was nothing better than a vengeful son, and a nigga who got cut out when he deserved to be on top. Cocaine knew what he needed to do.

"So, you gon' help a nigga out?" Cocaine asked as Wild Bill took out a cigar from his jacket and lit it. He was old school, and old school niggas smoked cigars.

"I don't even know where to look for them. I've been in every inch of the house; I don't know where they could be or how many there are. That's a suicide mission. If he finds out what we trnna do, he'll kill us, but shit, I don't give a fuck no more. I'm tired of workin' for a muthafucka that I really help put on. I'm sorry about that, Cocaine. Truly, I am. I ain't know he had a kid at the time, dude. I would never target a family man unless he wronged me, and he didn't. I didn't even know dude."

Cocaine accepted his apology wholeheartedly because he understood the loyalty Wild Bill was demonstrating. What he couldn't get behind was Dutch and how he was rockin'.

"So then, you down to help me, right? We gon' get back my father's legacy, I'ma take back over, and I'ma break bread with you. I know you tired of the game. I see it every time I look at you."

Wild Bill couldn't deny that. He was tired, and he was ready to move on. He was ready to go on about his business and retire somewhere on a beach, so he did the only thing he could do; he agreed, and thus, the plan to take down Dutch was born.

Wild Bill couldn't leave the party without saying goodbye to Lexxy, but he knew it was time to go, and although she'd forgiven Cocaine for what happened, he didn't think she'd be able to forgive him for what he was about to do.

It was time for Wild Bill to get his revenge. He deserved it, he wanted it, and it was only fair for him to have it.

Who the fuck did Dutch think he was by keeping all of that money away from Wild Bill? Really, it was more than that, so much more than that. He felt betrayed by the man who was supposed to be his friend. He didn't want him to be set for life, but he was livin' good while Wild Bill took the smallest amount of money every time.

That set up with Juaqeen was supposed to be a come up for both of them. It was Wild Bill who told Dutch about it, but did he care? No. Did he show him any loyalty? No.

It was one thing after another, all the time, always.

Wild Bill knew if he was going to have to tell Lexxy goodbye, he couldn't do it sober. He needed some liquid courage to tell his sweet Lexxy the truth of the matter, and he had to tell her what the deal was.

He went to the bar and grabbed a drink. Cocaine had even hired a bartender for the event; Wild Bill's drink of choice was always Bourbon, and he needed at least a double shot to get him started.

Before long, Wild Bill was getting wasted. He wasn't a violent drunk, but he was loud. The music had started flowing through his body, and he was dancing with all of the women there, including Denise who was also drunk out of her mind, but they needed this. The release from the stress they were starting to feel was what they all needed, even if they didn't know it. This party wasn't just for Lexxy; it was also for the many people who loved her. The people who had supported her through this time.

Her coworkers had been so good to her during this time, and they really missed her. They weren't sure if she'd ever be able to make it back to work, but they were just happy to be able to spend this time with her. Though Lexxy wasn't able to have a drink, she was still on cloud nine. She was now back in her wheelchair like she agreed she would, and she was wheeling around the party, enjoying her guests.

As the party continued, people started leaving, and as the house emptied, Wild Bill figured this was his time to say what he needed to.

Denise was too drunk to move, so Cocaine had set her up on the other side of the house so she could sleep it off. She turned up way too hard, and at one point, was yelling to everyone, "I'm the queen around this bitch," and that was when Lexxy told Cocaine to help her to the other room. When people started leaving, she didn't want her best friend to be caught up trying to drive home and fuck around and hurt herself.

Wild Bill put down his Bourbon and went over to Lexxy; it was time for him to say goodbye.

With alcohol dripping from his pores and sweat falling from his forehead, he was finally ready to let it all go.

"Lexxy, I need to talk to you."

Lexxy turned her head and saw Wild Bill approaching her. She spun around on her wheels and saw him, and she knew he had had too much to drink.

"Oh, Unc, whatever it is, wait until you're sober. You look too through."

"No, Lex-Lexxy, I-I gotta tell you now," Wild Bill said as he was beginning to choke up.

Lexxy noticed the tears that were surfacing, and she knew whatever it was, it was serious.

"Ok, what's up? What's going on?" She extended her hand out to touch Wild Bill's, and he cracked. He completely broke down.

"I'm only one man, Lexxy. I got feelings too. I got shit that I'm supposed to be doing, that I've always wanted to do, and it ain't right what your father did to me." Wild Bill took a sip of a nearby beer that was laying on the table.

"Your father robbed me of my chance at success. I'll never work my way up. I'll always be stagnant if I don't handle his ass, so I'm telling you right now, I'm done with your father and his shit. I ain't got time to be dealin' with him no mo'. I've done all I could do, I've been a good friend to that nigga, and this is the thanks I get? Cut out of the deal that I helped that nigga even come up on? Nah, I gotta get rid of that nigga. He's like a fuckin' plague. He's ruined so many lives, and I'm 'bout to take his. The only reason I'm tellin' you is because I didn't want it to be a surprise, and I love you so much, I just know you won't be able to forgive me after what I'm about to do."

Lexxy's hand covered her eyes. She didn't want to cry, but how could she not? Wild Bill, her only uncle was leaving her, and even though she was angry, and she wanted to tell him no, she knew she couldn't change his mind. Drunk words were always sober thoughts, and the best thing she could do was wish him well.

Unfortunately, her father had raised her in the game. He'd prepped her for situations such as this; the day where friend became foe, family becomes enemy, but it was all his fault. It was his doing, and as badly as Lexxy wanted to tell him there was another way, she knew deep down that there wasn't, just like she knew there was no way to stop Cocaine, and if they were teaming up, they would be unstoppable.

She rose from her wheelchair steadily, propping herself up on the handles of the chair. Her legs were weak from all the walking she'd done that day, and she was glad to have a wheelchair at this point to rely on.

Just like when she was a little girl, she wrapped her arms around Wild Bill's neck and clung tightly to him. She didn't know if this was the last time she was going to see him, but she knew for sure that the next time she did see him, her father would be dead, and she didn't even blame him. She knew the hard work Wild Bill had put in over the years, she knew when he was in prison that it was so her father didn't have to be.

He killed a man for her father, and countless other men, so that her father could stay on the streets and reign supreme, but what had her father given back? Absolutely nothing. He'd given Wild Bill nothing as an appreciation, he'd given him nothing to fall back on. Wild Bill wasn't living paycheck to paycheck, and he wasn't really hurting financially, but there was more for him; there was more than what this life had offered him previously.

Wild Bill couldn't hold on for long; for one, he was fucked up, and for two, his heart broke with every second that passed by that he had Lexxy on him.

He removed her arms from around him and told her how much he loved her, and he hoped that one day, she would come around, that this wouldn't ruin their relationship forever.

"I love you, Unc. I'm so, so sorry."

"It's not your fault, baby. I love you too, Lexxy."

Wild Bill stumbled out of the house. Lexxy didn't want him drinking and driving, but he'd done it plenty of times, and Wild Bill knew how to handle himself. If he couldn't drive, he would've said something. That was one thing she loved about him. If he couldn't do something, he didn't have a problem saying it. Though he was a cold-hearted killer, he was human, and Lexxy respected that about him. He didn't act like he was indestructible like her father. That nigga thought he was a god, but a god didn't have to say it a million times. A god was a god, and he earned the respect of his people. Instead, Dutch's people feared him. They feared what he was capable of…what he had done in the past, and where he was leading people to.

Several Months Later…

Cocaine and Lexxy had been together for a year now, and though things were hard, they weren't terrible. The doctor had given them the ok to have sex as long as it wasn't too rough or too strenuous, and Cocaine had been waiting for this moment to come. Sure, he was horny, but he mainly missed the intimacy he needed to feel with his woman.

It was their anniversary, and Cocaine couldn't wait to celebrate. He'd never had an anniversary to celebrate or think about other than his father's death. He didn't even celebrate his own birthday, which would be coming up soon, but he didn't want to do anything special for it. He just wanted more time with his woman.

Cocaine knew Lexxy wasn't going to want to get out, and it really wasn't a good idea to. She had started becoming short of breath whenever she walked too long, or any time she wasn't in the bed really, but tonight, he made special plans for his beautiful woman. He was going to make her his forever, and not just with words. Tonight was all about Lexxy. He'd enlisted the help of

Denise and Junie so that everything would go smoothly for the night.

Lexxy often felt she wasn't as beautiful as she once was, but Cocaine didn't see that. When he looked at her, he still saw the beautiful girl he'd met at the diner a year ago. He saw his Sexxy Lexxy, his doctor woman. He was proud of Lexxy, and though she couldn't do much these days, that didn't matter to him. All he asked was that she love him and love him she did. She loved him with her entire being, and now, he was going to seal that love with a ring.

That morning, Cocaine snuck out of the house so that Junie and Denise could come over and help Lexxy get ready, and hopefully get her in the mood for the night.

She'd said previously that she didn't want to do anything because emotionally, she wasn't feeling up to it, but fuck that. He had plans, and she was just gonna have to deal with that.

Before he left, he left her a written note on his side of the bed so she wouldn't panic when she woke up, which she often did whenever Cocaine wasn't there. She always would relive the moment she came home to find all of Lucky's things gone, and even though this was Cocaine's house, it wasn't unheard of for a nigga to run away from home. That shit happened all the time.

Lexxy rolled over in the bed as soon as she saw the shadow in the room that was cast from the sun. It was beautiful. The rays shone on her like diamonds sparkling in the sky.

Immediately, she noticed Cocaine wasn't there, but

before she had time to even get upset, she felt the envelope in the bed. With a quickness, she grabbed it and opened it up, pulling the note out of the inside.

"Good morning, Sexxy Lexxy, I stepped out for a few…your mom and Denise are in the living room waiting for you to get up, so when you feel up to it, go on out there and make an appearance, don't make them come in there and get you. I love you, and I won't be gone long. BTW, happy anniversary, beautiful. One year down, but we got forever to go."

Lexxy didn't have forever, and though nobody did, that didn't make her feel any better. It didn't make her feel good to know that her man was still hoping that they'd be able to spend a lifetime together when they really didn't have that much time left. According to the doctor, Lexxy should be dead already, and she wasn't, but it could happen at any moment. She could drop dead at any second, and she knew that.

She didn't want to see her mother or Denise, not right now, and definitely not today. She really just wanted to mourn her anniversary. Sure, she was alive for this one, but would she live long enough to see the next one?

Her hair had begun falling out from stress, her face grew stress lines in them, and she didn't feel like a young woman anymore. She felt like an old, sick hospital patient.

But she knew she couldn't avoid them forever, and Denise wasn't above coming in her room and jumping on the bed, sick or not, Denise was childish.

Lexxy worked her way out of the bed and into her chair. She'd gotten pretty good at getting herself in and out of it now. When she was firmly seated in the chair, she wheeled herself into the living room and ran right into her mother and Denise who were drinking mimosas.

"Good morning, sunshine!" her mother yelled.

"Bestie! Yasss.....I'm so glad you finally woke up. We got a lot of shit planned! Ladies, come on out."

Lexxy hadn't even brushed her teeth yet, but she figured she didn't have to; she was with family, but now, this bitch was talkin' to other people? What did they really have going on?

Lexxy looked toward the back of the house, and out came racks of clothes, women with make up smocks on, a woman with a flat iron and a whole station of shit.

"Uhm...what is all of this?" Lexxy asked, curious as to what the answer would be.

"This is for you. Since you're not supposed to really be out and about, we brought it to you. Today is your anniversary, and we can't have you lookin' all dusty and shit. The bestie I know would want to look her best, and that's what you're gonna have, the best of everything today."

Lexxy wished she was in a better mood to truly appreciate what was happening around her, but she just wasn't, and of course, her mother realized it.

"Alexxis, I know that you're not feeling like yourself, like the world is out to get you because of this sickness, baby, but you gotta push through it. You gotta live for today and worry about tomorrow, tomorrow. You can't let this kill you before it's your time, baby. You have such a vibrant personality and so much love to give, but you can't be afraid to live because you're afraid to die. You'll miss too much of your life doing so."

Even though Lexxy wasn't supposed to be drinking, at least on most occasions, her doctor said since it was her anniversary, a few glasses wouldn't hurt. Plus, she wasn't showing signs of progression or regression, which was neither good nor bad, but it was better than bad news.

Her mother handed her an orange filled glass and told her to chug it.

"Drink up, my dear, the best is yet to come."

Lexxy snatched that glass from her mother so quickly. It seemed like it had been forever since she tasted the bitter taste of alcohol, and she missed it.

After two mimosas, she felt better, and she was ready to get her day started.

The women began their pampering session by getting their nails done, and then they moved on to their hair, and by the end, they had picked out the perfect dress for Lexxy to wear for the evening.

"This is beautiful, but I can't even stand up long enough to wear heels, there's no point in a pretty dress if I can't wear nice shoes to match." Lexxy pouted.

"Uhn-uhn....that's not true, hold up."

Denise had told the woman about Lexxy's condition and how she was pretty much wheelchair bound. She knew her best friend wasn't going to want to wear stilettos in a chair, so she asked the designer ladies to bring her something that would be fashionable but comfortable, and something that would still make her feel very feminine.

Denise reached under the clothes racks and grabbed

a pair of sparkly flip flops, custom made just for her, and they matched her dress perfectly.

"Denise, what are those?"

"These, dear sister, are your shoes. They can be worn for leisure, or for special occasions like tonight. Now, don't question me. Go get dressed, put those on, and wait for your man to come home. He's definitely gon' be slangin' that dick tonight! Ehhh!" Denise yelled with her tongue out.

Junie just shook her head. She loved Denise because she was fun, but she could go a little overboard sometimes.

"So, that's it? Y'all are leaving?"

Before Lexxy knew it, the day had gone by, and it was well in the afternoon.

"Yes ma'am, it's your anniversary, not ours. Enjoy yourself, and don't think too much about it. Cocaine should be back in about an hour, so take your time getting dressed. Your hair is slayed with the bundles, bitch, your make up is beat to the gods, and not even Cardi B can compete with those nails tonight, baby!"

Lexxy knew her best friend was trying to pump her up to make her feel better, and for once, it was actually working.

Lexxy said her goodbyes to all the ladies who helped make her day special, including her mother and Denise, and then she went back into her room to get dressed.

She had no idea what the night held for her and Cocaine, she just hoped he would be pleased with her and that her attitude didn't ruin their magical evening that was ahead.

Cocaine came home finally after a long day of getting shit done. He wanted the day to be special for Lexxy, and there were still so many things he had to do when he left the house, but as long as the ring came through, he didn't give a damn about the rest for real.

For the last several months, Cocaine had been looking for the rest of his family. He never knew both of his grandparents, just his grandmother, but DNA was a motherfucker and it could link you up with your people if you had the funds, and Cocaine certainly did.

He went around the globe trying to find this people, and when he did, he went all the way back to Texas, on a damn day trip to get something very special.

He remembered as a little boy his father telling him about the giant diamond ring his mother wore that his pops had given her, and Cocaine dreamed of that ring. Though he'd never seen the ring, he figured it must've been special for her to keep wearing it even after his grandfather left his grandmother, but it was an heirloom and he wanted his Lexxy to have it because she was all the family he had left.

Upon finding his grandmother and introducing herself, she was under the impression Juaqeen never had any children, but she said he probably distanced himself because of the lifestyle he led, and there was no way he was gonna see something happen to his own mother.

But she received Cocaine with open arms, though she would have liked for his name to not be Cocaine it was entirely too late to change it at this point.

Cocaine went down there with intent and told his grandmother what he wanted, and to his surprise, she gave it up willingly. She didn't put up a fight. She'd always wished she had someone to hand it down to, and now she did. She said it was a burden she'd carried with her most of her life because she wouldn't dare pawn it and see it end up in the wrong hands. Some things belonged with family, and she was happy to have some of that now since she'd been living all alone for some time now.

Cocaine had to have the ring sized, and he was just thankful that it was finally ready for today. He swung by the jeweler, the mall to get his tailored suit, and of course the flower shop to get Lexxy all the tulips she could ever want. There were one hundred in the order he placed, and he didn't want to have them delivered in case she was asleep, so he picked them up himself and brought them home.

When he made it to the house, he snuck in through the back and admired the handy work of Junie and Denise. If things went according to plan, Lexxy had no idea what was waiting for her in the back of the house.

Cocaine called Lexxy on her phone to see if she was almost ready, and he thought she was probably sleep or still needed time, but no, she was all the way together. Cocaine told her to meet him in the dining room in ten minutes. That was all he needed.

The tulips were sitting in the middle of the table of the dining room, courtesy of his helpers around the house that he'd hired once he brought Lexxy home to keep an eye on her. He put on his suit and slid the ring in his pocket.

He was finally ready.

Before he left the back room, he went to turn his phone on silent because he didn't want any interruptions, but when he did, he saw a missed call from Trisha. She couldn't have been calling at a worse time. He'd called her days ago to get some intel on Dutch, but she hadn't called him back yet. He figured it would take her a few days but damn, it had been like a week now, but that wasn't important today. Today was all about Lexxy, so he proceeded to cut his phone on silent, and he slid his phone back in his pocket.

When he came out of the room and into the dining room, Lexxy's beautiful dress and the smile she wore lit up the room.

"Happy anniversary, handsome, she said as she reached into the table to pick a tulip.

"They're beautiful baby. Thank you."

"Not nearly as beautiful as you. I done hit the damn jack pot."

Cocaine came around the table and kissed his soon to be fiancé, and he took a second to admire her, and everything about her. She was truly a sight to see.

"So, what do you have planned for tonight?" she asked inquisitively.

"I guess you'll just have to wait and see, but first, let's have dinner."

Lexxy rolled herself over to her seat, and with no help, she was able to get into the dining room chair, and she did it effortlessly. Not a hair fell out of place.

When Lexxy was comfortable, Cocaine grabbed the small remote that sat on the table, and he hit play. Soon after, the sweet sounds of Miles Davis, Lexxy's favorite musician, played through the speakers.

Lexxy smiled, realizing how amazing Cocaine was. The room was decorated in lavender and yellow, Lexxy's two favorite colors. The chandelier above them had petals falling from them, as if it was snowing flowers, but it wasn't distracting.

Cocaine reached for her hand and waited for the night to continue to unfold.

He hired a professional chef to cook for them, and the food had been done for hours, and Denise saw to it that she didn't even know about the food because Lexxy could eat, and if she knew some good food was in the house, she wouldn't hesitate to smash it.

Three men dressed in coat tail tuxedos came out, holding food, drinks, and desserts. Cocaine didn't want it brought out one by one because he knew his baby could eat, and if she wanted dessert first, she could have it tonight.

As they uncovered the trays of grilled salmon and asparagus, molten chocolate lava cake, and mashed potatoes with rice underneath, which was Lexxy's favorite, her mouth began watering.

"Look at you ole fat ass," Cocaine said jokingly.

"I'm just playing, baby, eat up."

The night they were having was a magical one, and it was beautifully planned. Everything was coming together perfectly, but Cocaine was tired of waiting. He couldn't take it anymore.

As the music played and Lexxy ate her food, Cocaine started a conversation with her that was ultimately going to lead her into the trap of saying yes.

"So, Sexy Lexxy, you think you'll marry me one day?"

She looked up from her food with a weird face.

"Cocaine, we had this talk. Let's see how things go after the transplant. Besides, I don't know what kind of ring I want or even what kind of wedding I want."

"I,I, I, huh? What about me? Let me tell you what I would want. I would want your fine ass to be eating dinner under a chandelier of falling tulips, listening to the sweet, undeniable sounds of Miles Davis. I would want you to look and feel at your best, and worry about tomorrow, tomorrow. Damn, that's happening right now ain't it?"

Lexxy giggled out of nervousness. She hoped Cocaine wasn't about to propose because she wasn't ready, not because she didn't love him but because she was dying. She didn't want to leave him before they even had a chance to get married.

Cocaine slid down on the floor, and Lexxy swallowed hard. Her food felt stuck in her throat, but so did her heart.

"Lexxy, I ain't the mushy type so don't give me a hard time, but you know I love you. You know I became whole the day I met you. This year has been one crazy fuckin' ride, lil' baby, but I wouldn't have it no other way. I don't wanna hear shit about you being sick and dying cuz if that's the case, you goin up out of here as my wife!"

Cocaine took the ring from his jacket pocket and slammed it down on the table.

"Now listen, you know you done made me a gentle soul, but if you say no, I might just kill you cuz I can't take no heartbreak, woman, so what's it gon' be? You gon' be mine, or what?"

Cocaine opened the box, and the giant diamond sparkled all over the room. Lexxy's mouth fell wide open in amazement.

She covered her mouth and didn't know what to say. She rose from her chair with doubt in her eyes, and Cocaine saw what her answer was going to be, but not tonight. She wasn't going to deny him and ruin his life.

"So I see I'ma have to make you act right," Cocaine said as tension built up in the room.

He knocked everything in his way on the table to the floor and picked Lexxy up and placed her on the table.

"Cocaine, what are you doing?"

She didn't know if she should be alarmed or turned on.

Cocaine pulled her dress up, revealing the fact that she had on no panties. He couldn't get his pants down fast enough.

His dick teased the lips of her pussy, which were now begging him to enter her.

Cocaine slid his dick deep inside of Lexxy. He put his hand around her neck and began choking her, not hard but rough, rough enough for her to like it. They weren't supposed to be doing this; it was against the doctor's orders, but she was out of her mind if she thought she was going to tell him no.

As he thrust in and out of her, he asked one simple question, “Will you marry me?”

She said nothing, or at least nothing that could be made out as words. She was too busy enjoying the dick.

“Will. You. Marry. Me?” he asked again, his dick beating her guts down.

He looked her in the eyes, and asked once more, her brain feeling like it would explode from the banging of his dick.

“Yass! Yes, I’ll marry you.”

She couldn’t believe she’d said it herself but there was no time to stop what they were doing. They made love on that table for what seemed like hours, and when they were finally done, Cocaine slid his grandmother’s ring on her finger, and ended the night how it should have been.

“I love you, Lexxy.”

“I love you too, Coco.”

They lie there, naked on the table, eating the chocolate dessert from one another’s mouths and bodies and truly enjoyed their one-year anniversary.

CHAPTER 31

Cocaine wished he could bask in Lexxy's love for the rest of his life, but the truth was he had shit to do, and it needed to be done now while the plan was fresh. Wild Bill had been playing the part, acting as if everything was good between him and Dutch, simply so he could find what he was looking for. It took him two weeks, but he finally found them.

Hidden in the backyard, where a part of the ground looked and felt different, Wild Bill found where the golden bricks were buried. See, Wild Bill was a real hood nigga, but he was also country. He paid attention to the patterns in the ground, and he knew when something wasn't right about the grass, and he'd found it.

With the help of Trisha, he was able to distract Dutch long enough for Wild Bill to even be able to find the bricks, but he couldn't dig them all the way up that day. That would've taken too long, so they made a plan, and they had to stick to it; they just had to figure out how they were going to be able to make this plan work.

Wild Bill filled Cocaine in on the deal and let him know what was to come. Trisha had been working for Dutch for a little over four years now, but she wasn't loyal to him. She had her own motives, but that's another story for another time.

That night she fucked Cocaine, she knew her life was about to change, and she was just glad that she was able to find the come up. She'd put in a lot of work for Dutch in a short amount of time, and she wasn't given the proper respect she deserved, and they had her fucked up if they didn't think she was going to get hers one way or another. Revenge was always lurking around Dutch whether he knew it or not.

Several days later, they figured out that Dutch wasn't going to be home, so this was the perfect time for them to dig up the back yard. After further consideration, they decided they wouldn't kill Dutch unless they had to, but them taking those bricks was going to start a war that they probably weren't prepared for, no matter how tough or rough the three of them were.

Trisha was crafty, very. She knew there was only one thing that could make Dutch run out of his home quickly, and that was fucking with his money. She knew that count day was coming, and Dutch trusted his men to make sure the money count was perfect, but she knew how to tamper with that shit, and that's what she did. She took some of the money from the trap houses that whole week, hoping the count would be off. She knew it was just a matter of time before Dutch came down from his palace to handle business, and when he did, the three of them would be ready.

Cocaine kissed Lexxy goodbye and told her he loved her. She didn't think anything about it, today was just a normal day to her. Every day Cocaine left. He was a "working" man, so she knew he would be out all day like most days, but she didn't mind. Though she was apprehensive to get engaged, she now loved looking at her ring every day as a daily reminder that she had someone who loved her, someone who wanted her forever, no matter how long that was going to last.

As soon as Dutch left the house, Wild Bill told Trisha, and Trisha told Cocaine, and they met at Dutch's house an hour or so later.

Instead of driving, they went on foot, it was safer and much easier. They could go undetected.

When they got in the backyard, Wild Bill was already in the back, scooping up the ground with a shovel.

"Dig!" he said as he threw them both shovels. Trisha hadn't planned on doing anything. She had already done her part, and getting dirty wasn't on her list of to-do's today. Cocaine promised to break both Trisha and Wild Bill off, and he was going to. When he made a promise, he planned to keep it.

The further they got into the ground, the gold practically beamed from underneath the surface. They were so close to victory.

Cocaine thought about what he would do once he got his legacy back and what he and Lexxy could accomplish with the hatred of his past gone.

Wild Bill wanted nothing more than to get gone and get ghost. He wanted to pretend that none of this ever happened. He could taste the freedom on his tongue.

Finally, the gold was in arm's reach, and Wild Bill put his arm in the hole to pull it out, but it couldn't be that simple, could it?

The loud sound of clicking alerted the three of them. No one thought to have anyone keep guard, and now they were caught.

"What the fuck is going on out here?" Dutch asked with two guns pointed at the three of them.

In Cocaine's mind, he felt like they could rush his ass and take him, but he didn't know if Wild Bill and Trisha were willing to take that chance.

Wild Bill stepped up and got in Dutch's face.

"For so long, for so fuckin' long I've stood by your side and watched you fuck some shit up, and I did it with you gladly because you were my friend, but then, I find out that my friend, a man I considered family, fucked me over and screwed me out of a deal I told him about! That's some bullshit, so if you have even a shred of decency left inside of you, you'll just let us take this shit and be on our way."

Dutch was about to speak, but Cocaine's phone rang, interrupting the commotion. It was Lexxy's home worker. He couldn't ignore that call.

"Hello?"

"What?"

"Ok, I'm on the way."

"Nah, nigga, you ain't goin' nowhere."

"Nigga, if you love your daughter, you gon' let me go. She's on the way to the hospital. She collapsed, bleeding from the mouth. This shit can wait."

Cocaine knew Dutch probably wasn't going to let him go, so Wild Bill rushed him, distracting him long enough to let Cocaine get away. He had to get to the hospital to get to his baby.

While Wild Bill and Dutch were wrestling on the ground, Trisha stuck her hand in the hole, trying to get as many bricks out as she could before they noticed what she was doing, but Dutch was hip to her, and he still had one bullet in his gun.

He fired a shot and shot Trisha directly in the leg. He wasn't going to kill her; she was one of the best female workers he had, and it came in handy to keep a couple of females on the team.

Shooting Trisha gave Wild Bill the second he needed to get the gun out of his hands. He was much stronger than Dutch.

He knocked the gun away from him, and climbed on top of him, and with his fists clenched, he began punching him, and punching him….before long, Dutch's lights would be out, and they would be able to get the gold and carry on with their plan.

Lexxy was at home, enjoying her day, and she knew

her year had come. She could feel it inching its way inside of her body, but she fought it. She fought it as long as she could. Her kidney, the one she had left, was failing her, and it hemorrhaged inside of her.

Cocaine and Lexxy both feared the same thing—not seeing each other one last time.

The sirens wailed around Lexxy, and even though she knew she couldn't hear him, it was probably her mind just playing tricks on her…but she could've sworn she heard Cocaine saying, "I'm on the way, baby. Don't leave me."

She would hang on as long as she could, but she didn't have long, and with no hope of a transplant, she was surely going to die.

Junie was supposed to be away on business, and she was almost gone, but when Cocaine called her, letting her know about Lexxy, she was already on her way home. She'd left something at home, and it made her change her mind about taking the trip in the first place.

When she got into the house, she saw the back door was wide open, which was strange, so she went outside to see what was happening.

As she got closer to the door, she could hear loud noises bursting through her ears.

She ran outside to see what was going on, and she saw Dutch on top of Wild Bill with a gun to his head, ready to blow his brains out.

"What you thought this was, nigga? Baby, go back in the house, I don't want you to see this."

Junie's stomach began to turn, and she couldn't help herself, she threw up.

"Don't you move, nigga!"

"Dutch, get off him, we have to get to the hospital. Whatever this is about can wait!"

"No, it can't wait. My own best friend runnin' 'round tryna betray me. I can't have that, baby."

"Do you hear me? Lexxy collapsed, we have to go!"

"I don't give a damn about that right now!"

He had Wild Bill right where he wanted him, and he was ready to pull the trigger, but the words that came out of Junie's mouth next changed their worlds forever.

"You can't kill him, Dutch! He's Lexxy's father."

As soon as the words left her mouth, she ran into the bathroom and finished yakking her guts up. The secret she'd been keeping Lexxy's entire life was finally out, and there was nothing she could do to pull it back in or change it. It was true.

Lexxy's real father was Wild Bill, and now, he might be Lexxy's only chance of having her life saved….

TO BE CONTINUED……

Follow me on social mediaaaaaaa!

tIKTOK: https://www.tiktok.com/@authornastee?_t=8oKW9zpRqcY&_r=1

FACEBOOK: https://www.tiktok.com/@authornastee?_t=8oKW9zpRqcY&_r=1

Facebook group: https://www.facebook.com/share/8XUtwdsL8SdE7EXN/

iNSTAGRAM: https://www.instagram.com/makeitnastee_?igsh=MWcwY3M5OHgxZDM0Mw%3D%3D&utm_source=qr

www.ingramcontent.com/pod-product-compliance
Ingram Content Group UK Ltd.
Pitfield, Milton Keynes, MK11 3LW, UK
UKHW041841190726
13854UKWH00002B/657